Witches in Dreamland

Witches in Dreamland

A Novel by David Barker and W. H. Pugmire

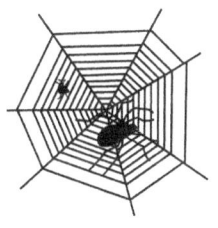

Hippocampus Press

New York

Acknowledgment

The authors want to express appreciation to Craig Klyver for his expert advice about the techniques used by professional paper conservators and book restorers. The insights thus gained helped greatly during the writing of scenes set at Miskatonic University's Orne Library.

Published by Hippocampus Press
P.O. Box 641, New York, NY 10156.
http://www.hippocampuspress.com

Hippocampus Press logo by Anastasia Damianakos.
Cover design and restoration of vintage illustration by Dan Sauer, dansauerdesigncom

First Edition
1 3 5 7 9 8 6 4 2

ISBN 978−1−61498−230−2

PROLOGUE

She was a petite and elderly woman dressed in a simple black gown that reached to her ankles. Her shimmering white hair, brushed back, reached to her waist and moved in the night wind. One hand grasped an unornamented black walking stick; and it was curious that, despite this assistant of wood, the woman possessed a sense of strength and fortitude that was most notable in her handsome face. The face contained a remnant of beauty; yet it was a morbid loveliness, for the facial flesh was of so thin a nature that one could almost discern the skull beneath the features. It was because of this morbid aspect of her countenance that people sometimes spoke of her as Madame Death. Her dark green eyes examined the multitude of stars that adorned the midnight sky spreading over the venerable church that was her destination, and she enjoyed the way those chilly stars seemed to taint an element of the night air to such a degree that she could taste its quality on her tongue.

An odd chiming sounded and returned her attention to St. Toad's. "How magnificent to see you again, old friend," she whispered. "Your black spire looms beneath the stars as of old, and the small square windows below your peaked roofs are black and lightless. You seem to be sleeping, but I know that you are keenly aware, and waiting. I come to knock upon your large brass doors and pass through your threshold. Allow me entrance."

The small woman advanced and climbed the three roughhewn stone steps that led to the massive doors, against one of which she thumped the handle of her walking stick. There was a slight pause, as if night were holding its breath; and then the doors opened inward and the woman's nostrils drank in the flow of perfumed air that is—sued from the edifice. She saw the shrouded figure whose head was concealed with an enormous hood; and although the too—large lump that was the creature's head was hidden, she knew from the mon—strous hand that held a lantern that the creature was inhuman. The figure stooped in genuflection and spoke her name.

"We welcome your return, Edith Gnome. How is it that we may assist you?"

"I've come to collect some water from the fount of tears. Lead the way, please."

The bent hooded creature swayed slightly, held its lantern high—er, and turned from the woman. She followed it through corridors and archways, over the floor that was sometimes stone and some—times of a pattern of red and black tiles. Their way was lighted by some few primitive chandeliers in which squat yellow candles burned. At last they came to the antique fount that stood almost five feet in height, and the woman bent over the basin and gazed at the chiseled faces of pale stone beneath the water. From a pocket in her dress she produced a slim green bottle and removed its stopper, and then she lowered the bottle to the bottom of the basin. She moaned slightly as one of the stone faces opened its mouth and pressed its lips against the fabric of her hand. Something in the kiss was so forlorn that the woman could not stop the tears that filled her eyes and dropped silently into the basin. At last she lifted her slim green bottle out of the water and replaced its stopper. Her companion studied her in silence and then raised a sallow inhuman hand on which a ring of white gold encircled one misshapen finger. Taking the creature's hand into her own, she brought it to her mouth, shut her eyes, and kissed the ring.

The perfumed air transfigured and took on a different scent, one that was sweet and slightly cloying. When at last she opened her eyes, Edith Gnome saw that she no longer stood in a church that existed in rare dreamland; rather, she stood in the strange woodland of Sesqua Valley.

CHAPTER I

Agnes Aspinwall raised her head and opened her mouth so that the falling snow touched her lips and tongue. The woodland of Sesqua Valley was absolutely silent, and the darkness of night hid its trees from view. Shivering a little, the young woman turned to retrace her foot−steps in the snow that led to Edith Gnome's cottage, which stood near the main business section of Sesqua Town. Reaching the door, she stood for some moments in the doorjamb and watched the snow a lit−tle longer; and then she opened the door and stepped into the cottage, where the unexpected sight of Edith's night−time visitor confronted her. Edith's smile, as she looked at her friend, was almost apologetic.

Edith shrugged. "Simon could smell anticipated magick, and so here he is, to investigate. I've never known anyone whose senses are so keen."

The ugly fellow smiled and looked down at the elderly woman, over whom he towered as they stood side by side. "Your magick has a peculiar stink, seeing that you are an Arkham witch. I always grow a little leery when you vacate your homeland and infiltrate our town."

"My alchemy is as much a part of Sesqua Valley as it is of witch−haunted Arkham. I have been molded by both realms."

Agnes closed the door and walked to the center of the room. "What is it about Arkham that nauseates you so, Simon? One would think you'd feel quite at home there."

"It's because he feels excluded from our charmed circle," Edith opined. She gazed at Simon as she continued. "I've never known anyone so shunned as this fellow. He's tainted, you see, from having memorized every known edition of the *Necronomicon,* a feat that has so distorted his soul that several realms reject his fellowship. I've even heard it whispered that he cannot enter the dreamland of men because of his corrupt nature."

"You listen to a lot of prattle," Simon sneered as he lowered the rim of his hat halfway over his silver eyes. "No matter. I want to know what's going on. I am attuned to the valley's senses—she and I know when something outré is afoot. You never dwell here, hag, unless you're up to something, in need of alchemy that you cannot conjure in your dull New England town. Who is your friend here, and what are the two of you plotting?"

Agnes pretended to smile. "Are you the mayor, that you demand such interference in private matters? Have we broken the rules of your jurisdiction?"

"I am the first—born beast of this valley," Simon answered.

Edith laughed. "Yes, you are a potent fellow indeed, pregnant with a sense of rule. And yet there are places in the valley that you do not violate, pockets that repel you. The place in the woodland where the trees of Sesqua Valley join the forests of dreamland, for example, is a setting that unsettles you. You hate being excluded from haunts of powerful magick in which you find no foothold, which is why you hate Arkham witchery."

"I know of no one who has penetrated into the forests of dream—except you. Is that what you're about? Have you plans to summon the night—gaunts from their homeland, or conjure the shade of Nyarlathotep? Are you plotting to initiate this young crea—ture into the mysteries of dreaming?"

"As I did for you? Remember, Simon, it was I who taught you how to dream, however seldom you do so. I was the one wise enough to awaken your ability to step into dreaming and thus escape mundane reality."

"Little good it has done me," the beast complained to the small woman. "The dreams you have bequeathed me are such pallid things."

Edith shrugged. "There is a part of you, perhaps, that is afraid to dream fully; because in dreams one is often not allowed to organize events, and you cannot tolerate any loss of control. That is one of your tragic weaknesses, beast. Perhaps that is one further lesson I can teach you—the delicious experience of the anarchy of dreaming. One can experience it absolutely by stepping into dreamland."

Strolling to a nearby chair, Simon sat, leaned back, and folded his arms. "Well, it is as you say—I am unable to enter the realm of dreamland, because of my exquisite corruption."

Ah—the twinkle in Edith's eyes! "Only the dreamland of men and mortality. There are a multitude of dreamlands, and I know of one that you could enter easily enough, if so inclined. And that brings us to the reason why I have summoned this young woman to the valley. I mean to transport her into the dreamland of witchery."

Sarcastically, Simon blew air. "I've never heard of such a thing."

Ignoring Simon, Edith stalked toward Agnes and reached for the younger woman's hands. "There is an item that I want retrieved from the dreamland of witches—a key of shadow that may usher one into the spaces between dream and death. I hunger to learn the se‑ crets that may be whispered in such spaces. However, the tedious 'rules' of sorcery are such that I cannot fetch the key on my own—it must be obtained for me by another. You are young and strong, and I think you may be able to withstand the perils that haunt this dreamland of antique sorcerers and beldames. I can guide you to the threshold of dream, but once it is crossed you will be on your own." Here she slid her eyes toward Simon for one moment. "Unless there is one foolhardy enough to accompany you."

There was a moment of pregnant silence; and then Simon, his strange silver eyes gleaming, shrugged his wide shoulders. "Well, it is as you say. I am too deliciously 'corrupt' to enter the flimsy world of dreamland."

"Only the dreamworld of men, Simon. As a potent warlock, you could easily enter the dreamland of witchery." Edith peered steadily into his eyes. "With my assistance. Of course, you'll have to suc‑ cumb to a bit of Arkham alchemy."

The beast of Sesqua Valley wrinkled his nose at her, yet his strange eyes flashed with fascination. "The dreamland of witchery—bah! In all my studies I have never found mention of such a realm."

The elderly woman shrugged. "Very few know of it. It's a bit like your mysterious Sesqua Valley—it calls to some chosen few, yet rarely." In a flash, Edith darted from the room and entered her bed-room, and Simon frowned distastefully at the sound of her happy humming. When she reentered the living room, Edith held a pecu-liar-looking bottle and what looked to be a silver spoon with a han-dle shaped like a large and antique key.

Agnes reached for the bottle, took hold of it, and held it up to candlelight. "What strange colors it contains, and how strangely they swirl!" She eyed the silver spoon uncomfortably. "I'm not to drink it, presumably."

"Not much, for it is a potent potion. The spoon, as you see, is also a key—to dreamland, where it may indeed have been fashioned. With these, and my aid, you will be able to cross the threshold be-tween this waking world and the dreamland of witchery. Only we who are practitioners of the arcane arts can do so—if we have an in-tense and sincere desire for such crossing over."

"Will we exist as dreaming entities of no substance, or will we have some physical form?"

"I cannot say for certain, Agnes. Not that it matters. You will have abilities there that one cannot achieve in wakefulness. You will be able to locate the key of shadow and bring it to me. Will you?"

Agnes wrinkled her forehead. "How can I bring something from the dreamworld into our physical reality?"

Edith's voice was low and quiet. "Oh, it's been done before, willfully and by accident. But you must deeply desire to assist me." Edith motioned to the bottle. "Will you, my pet?"

Agnes held the bottle to her eyes and studied its cloudy contents once more. "I will."

CHAPTER II

They followed a path through the woodland on which there was but little snow, due to the canopy created by the overhanging branches of trees that grew so closely together. Edith had placed her bottle and spoon into a shoulder bag, and she was surprised, as they walked, that Simon didn't produce one of his enchanted flutes and begin to fill the woodland with uncanny music, as was his habit during those times when outlandish alchemy was about to be practiced in the valley. Simon was obviously preoccupied with the ideas that had been planted into his brain by Edith's mention of an alternative dreamland, and the promise of his being able to visit such a realm. He knew instinctively where they were headed and smiled as they approached the circle of seven gnome−like figures that had been created from old stone.

"Ah, the Circle of Seven Dreamers. A fitting place for dream−ritual, Gnome. I've never noticed before, how these goblins so resemble your sprite−like self. Indeed, this one could be your twin, it almost wears your face." The tall fellow knelt before one of the figures and smoothed his hand over its features. Simon's voice wore its usual haughty and superior tone, but his eyes could not conceal their troubled aspect. Looking at Edith, he realized that she understood his unease; and so he did his best to ignore her knowing expression and reached his hand out to Agnes. "Come, Aspinwall—join me in our circle of fate. Kneel next to me here, and let us allow this hag to work her alchemy."

The younger woman, smiling tenderly, smoothed her hand

against Edith's cheek; and then she stepped into the circle of stone
figurines, positioned herself next to the beast, and leaned so as to kiss
his forehead. Simon regarded Agnes with an expression of mild dis—
taste, and then his eyes surveyed the trees surrounding them. Lov—
ingly, Agnes pressed her palms to the ground on which they knelt
and summoned the magick of the valley; and after a little while its
manifestation came to her, in the subtle pulse that began to throb
from some deep place beneath them. She looked above them and
saw that the trees were leaning slightly toward their circle of en—
chantment, and she closed her eyes when some snouted thing on the
titanic white mountain nearby began to bay. Sesqua Valley loved
ritual and dreaming, and she would assist in the power evoked by
Edith Gnome, a power that would blend the dimension between re—
ality and dream.

The ancient woman placed her shoulder bag onto the ground
and removed the bottle and curiously shaped spoon from it; and, as
she held those items in one hand, she pressed her empty hand to the
ground and curled its fingers into the sod. "Sesqua welcomes our
enchantment and calls to our blood with its heartbeat. Take these,
Simon, and feed the elixir to Agnes. She will then offer the spoon to
you. Ah, Simon, how your silvery eyes shimmer in this gloom of
night! What wonders they will witness in a little while."

Agnes stared into Simon's fantastic eyes and relished his inhuman
nature. She knew that he was not born of woman but was a spawn
of the supernatural valley, a beast that had his origin in the shadow—
land of Sesqua Valley and had somehow found his way onto the
mortal plane. There were others of his kind to be found in Sesqua
Towne, recognized by their non—human qualities—the shape of
their faces and the outré chemistry of their near—alabaster eyes. Ag—
nes saw how those eyes glimmered excitedly as the fellow took the
bottle and spoon from Edith and poured a small portion of the elixir
into the spoon's bowl; and then she shut her own eyes as Simon lift—
ed the spoon to her mouth and pushed it between her lips. She knew
that the liquid had entered her mouth, and yet the sensation she ex—
perienced was more like a memory of taste than taste itself. She took

the items that Simon offered her and poured a small amount of the liquid into the spoon. Simon's eyes did not close but continued to gaze at Agnes as she brought the spoon to the beast's mouth.

The pulse of Sesqua Valley deepened in force, as from the surrounding woodland a mauve mist began to billow toward the occupants of the woodland. Simon watched that mist and frowned when he noticed the crimson tint that began to spill into it. He turned his eyes to Edith Gnome, as if she could explain the change in atmosphere; but she merely shook her head a little as her figure began to fade from view, replaced by fantastic sentient shadows that seemed to dance around the kneeling couple. Simon watched, mesmerized, as the billowing mist began to rise and the fantastic world to which they had been transitioned came into view; and his body shivered with uncommon emotion as, taking his companion's hands into his own, he breathed the enchanted aether of dreamland.

CHAPTER III

Mandy Peaslee's first trip to the dreamlands was purely accidental. She had never heard of the dreamlands and had no inclination or intention to visit such a strange and mysterious realm. Had she known about it and considered, even for a second, hazarding a trip there, she would have instantly decided against it. Too risky, too unpredictable. And to what purpose? Everything she wanted was in the waking world where, as a graduate student, she was learning the craft of book conservation at Miskatonic University's Orne Library under the tutelage of Professor Henry Ashley, the renowned expert in paper restoration. Why chance losing all she had worked for over the past six years of college on cheap thrills in some airy−fairy fantasy land? No way; the beaches of Waikiki were about as far as she wanted to venture on vacation.

But nobody asked her preference, and there was no warning of the impending adventure. One minute she was at home in bed on a Wednesday evening, propped up with pillows, reading a peculiar sonnet in a funky old book of poems she'd borrowed from the library collection, and the next minute she had nodded off and was blissfully unconscious. The book was a small volume of poetry written by an obscure Arkham author named Edith Gnome. Mandy had never heard of her, and she'd read widely in the regional literature of New England. Published in a limited edition in Boston in the 1920s, it was quite rare, according to the decidedly creepy guy—a fellow grad student—who had recommended the book to Mandy. "Old Edith was a well−known witch, and her verses are said to contain

secret coded information on the occult techniques she used to contact the spirit world." Mandy was sure this was a load of BS, but she
figured there might be some racy poems in the book—well, as racy
as literature could get in those days—as she'd once heard that all
modern witches are notorious free-love neo-hippie pagan types
who sleep with anyone and everyone.

What came next was more vision than dream. Most of her
dreams were dreary affairs: rehashes of the day's work with nothing
more exciting in them than battles against the bureaucracy, tools that
malfunctioned, and materials that would not cooperate. It seemed as
if in almost every dream she was trying to do her work-study thing,
there had been a change of management at the library, the conservation lab had been moved, she couldn't find her work space, Professor
Ashley was nowhere to be found, her papers were missing or in dis-
order, and absolutely no one would tell her what she was supposed
to be doing and where she was supposed to do it.

But this "dream"—or "vision"—was nothing like that. It was
fresh, raw, living experience, and vividly real. And she was not her
usual self—an unsociable, somewhat melancholy, mildly cynical
woman in her early twenties. It was as if she had miraculously re-
verted to an earlier incarnation, to a state of perfection where she
was eternally young, infinitely perfect, and completely free.

The vision was regretfully brief, lasting only a few moments, and
left her gasping, literally aching for more. If she could have died and
gone to live in that place, to be who she was in the vision, she would
have done it in a heartbeat. Screw Miskatonic U. and all the assholes
in the graduate program! This place—whatever it was—was far, far
better.

The images, the sounds, the sensations of it were indelibly etched
in her brain. She was a young girl of maybe thirteen or fourteen. A
lithe, sprite-like being with beautiful long, brown hair that fell to
her shoulders, clad in a simple white cotton gown that reached to
her ankles, her feet elegantly bare. And this was the weird part: she
was astride a giant phosphorescent moth, riding on its back through a
dark sky over a mysterious landscape. The region they were travers-

ing was not of this world—of that much she was sure. Just visible in the distance was a mountain range. Below her passed a featureless desert floor. The land and air were dimly lit, but not pitch−black, and their inherent colors—deeply muted—were the most gorgeous things she had ever beheld. The gargantuan moth's body parts were all different glow−in−the−dark hues: green, orange, yellow, blue, red, violet, and other shades she could not quite name—hues that were intensely rich but completely absent of warmth: cool, nocturnal tints. A soft, stubby fuzz covered these luminous body segments. Impossibly, the moth, whose back she rode like a unsaddled horse, seemed to be lighter than air. It effortlessly shot through the sky with hardly a stirring of its wings. She was hurling forward to some un− known destination, her hair thrashing madly behind her, her eyes stinging from the chill wind, and she had no fear, no cares, no desires at all. She was fully alive in that moment, doing what she was des− tined to do, with no thought of the past or the future. A young warrior waif on a quest to—what?

Never, ever in her life had she felt so damned good, so awe− somely beautiful, so gloriously free. Pure of heart, pure of mind, un− compromised.

And then the vision faded into the vacant nothingness of dream− less slumber, and she came awake, almost dropping the book in the process, and lifted her chin, which had drooped to rest upon her chest while she slept.

"Oh my," Mandy said out loud, although she was totally alone in the house. "Holy fuck! What was *that?*"

She picked up her phone from the nightstand and checked the time. It was late, after eleven. Three Facebook notifications and a missed call from her mother. She'd call her back in the morning. The last thing she wanted to hear before bedtime was a bunch of whining that her worthless dad was drunk again, or that her older sister was having another baby—as if three weren't enough already when you were a loser on food stamps. She turned off the phone, laid it on top of the closed book, and rolled over and assumed her favorite sleep position—on her right side with the blanket tucked up tight around the back of her neck.

★

The licorice–like flavor of the elixir still strong on their tongues, Simon and Agnes emerged from a murky, interdimensional mist and found themselves in the middle of a vast, featureless plain, walking side by side toward a distant mountain range. It was dark and gloomy all around, with absolutely no sign of civilization in any direction. It looked like the most remote desert imaginable.

"Oh . . . dear me. This isn't quite how I pictured the dreamland of witchery," Agnes murmured hesitantly. She worried about offending the Beast of Sesqua Valley. He seemed a bit of a hothead, this one, and frankly, she was more than a little afraid of him. She would have said no to the whole arrangement, told Edith that she wanted no part of this highly dubious deal; but it seemed the only way she would ever be able to visit the dreamland of witchery was to go along with Edith's plan, under the escort of this shady Simon person, and she did so very much desire to spend time in that magical realm. It would give her the chance to blossom fully in her calling, to come into her own. Really learning the Craft, becoming a genuine witch in the prosaic waking world of Arkham, Massachusetts, was more than merely a daily challenge; it was practically beyond the realm of possibility. The skeptics of all that is paranormal invariably assumed you were a deluded New Age lunatic if you so much as mentioned the non–material world, and the religious fundamentalists were all convinced you were the Devil's Bride or worse if they observed you invoking any spirit not endorsed by their theology. But in the dreamland of witchery, ah!—she could be herself there: free to revel in witchcraft without fear of unpleasant consequences from the neighbors. Free to study the Craft, to practice it openly and honestly among a community of like–minded thinkers. It would be absolutely delightful—she couldn't wait to begin. But the scene now before them—it was all wrong. This bleak wasteland was clearly not associated in any way with her beloved New England, in any dimension.

"Simon, are you certain we have actually arrived in the dream—land of witchery, as Edith promised we would, or could it be that we are simply dreaming in the mundane fashion, and we'll wake up soon—in separate chambers, of course!—feeling that we've been fools for daring to believe it possible to transition to that legendary realm?"

Simon looked at Agnes with an expression of unconcealed im—patience. Typical of his arrogance, he didn't bother to answer her. Instead, he bent over and picked up one of the countless small slips of paper that Agnes suddenly noticed were littering the ground in every direction. There were millions of them, and more: as many as there are grains of sand on a beach. Each slip of paper was the size of a medium Post—It note. A few words were printed on one side of the paper. With obvious pleasure, Simon handed it to Agnes and smirked.

"Here's your answer, Miss Aspinwall," he said haughtily. What an ugly being he was, she thought. Why on earth does Edith associ—ate with such an unpleasant creature? One should be more selective in choosing one's friends.

The words on the paper appeared to have been printed on an old—fashioned mimeograph machine, the kind used to duplicate school handouts decades ago when Agnes's mother was a child. She read it out loud, more for her own benefit than for Simon's.

"This is merely a transitional realm, through which you will pass in your journey to your ultimate destination."

She let it drop from her hand and stooped to pick up several more slips, reading each of them in turn:

"You will not remain here very long, and there's no good reason why you should remember this insignificant phase of your passage."

"Nothing here matters in the end; it is all illusion."

"Walk on, young seeker; a superior situation awaits you."

She let them all fall from her hands, one by one, feeling humili—ated and somehow cheated. Not only were the messages imprinted on these slips absurd, but the papers were unpleasantly soiled from their long contact with the desert floor. She brushed her hands to—

gether forcefully to remove the residual dust.

As if that were not bad enough, Simon was staring at her with unmasked disdain and shaking with obnoxious laughter. She decided he was a hopelessly uncouth person, irredeemably boorish and ill−mannered.

Gathering together what remained of her dignity, she walked on, ignoring his rudeness. Her mood suddenly shifted from irritation to wonderment as she noticed a far−off thing in the sky, something unexpectedly weird, even in a puzzling place like this. Was it an air−plane or a huge bird? It seemed more alive than mechanical, she mused. No, it was neither of those things. It lacked the sleek, streamlined silhouette of a jet, and its wings didn't seem to be mov−ing much, if at all. They were too still to be a bird's, given its speed. Maybe it was a large military drone. She had read about drones in the *Advertiser,* but had never seen one before.

Simon had also spotted the flying object and was studying it ap−prehensively. Perhaps he suspected an enemy had finally found him in this remotest of locations and was about to launch what must be a well−deserved assassination attack. As much as she would like to de−ny it, seeing him worry gave her a certain amount of satisfaction.

The mysterious, potentially hostile object was hurtling through the air with great speed and soon was close enough for them to make out what it actually was. Agnes was stunned. Irrational as it seemed, it was a tremendously large moth upon whose back rode a little girl in a white dress. This had to be the most beautiful moth she had ever seen, even more stunning than the rare tropical specimens kept pinned under glass in the Arkham Museum's natural history wing. Through some miracle of biochemistry, the insect actually glowed in the dark, creating a most magical effect. Agnes brought her hands together as if she were about to say a prayer, touched her fingertips to her lips, and gasped inaudibly. Now she was convinced this was no common dream. They were indeed in the dreamlands, on their way to a marvelous realm of universal witchery. Edith had achieved the desired goal. Agnes's habitually timid heart filled with luxuriant gladness as the girl astride the giant moth passed majestically over−

head. Even jaded Simon's mouth hung open with awe when he saw it. The taste of the elixir intensified and the scene before them dis−solved into a deep, black pool of oblivion.

CHAPTER IV

Simon and Agnes stood very still within a void of nothingness and silence; and then they noticed the single dot high above them, a point of reddish hue that began to expand as a sphere of crimson fire. "I believe," whispered Simon, "that is the moon over this particular dreamland." They continued watching and felt a coolness on their eyes, as if some cosmic wind had drifted to them from the orb in the sky; and then they noticed how the strengthening glow of the al‑chemical moon began to drench the scene around them, so that strange distant hills came into view, and beyond those hills a range of fantastic mountains. Noticing an exotic shrub near them, Simon went to it and touched his fingers to its green leaves and pink blos‑soms; and then he pinched one leaf from the shrub and placed it into his mouth. "I cannot tell if we inhabit this realm as physical entities or if we have left our corporeal shells behind in the waking world— but we have taste, we can eat, and I can feel the weight of my frame."

Simon turned to Agnes, expecting some kind of response, and was a little annoyed that she seemed to have forgotten his presence as her wonderstruck eyes drank in the surrounding vista through the lens of her eyeglasses. Stepping to the young woman, he touched her shoulder and smiled at her sudden jump.

"You surprise me, Aspinwall," Simon cooed. "One would think, with your family history, that you would find a dreamworld a natural habitat in which to dwell."

It was the woman's turn to laugh, quietly and sardonically.

"What could you possibly know of my family history, beast?"

"I know that your great-grandfather died mysteriously while trying to establish an apportionment of the Randolph Carter estate to his heirs—that happened in New Orleans. Was it in 1929? I've never been certain of the exact date. I know that his elder son, who worked with his father in Chicago, began to investigate the circum-stances of his sire's death—and this led to his gathering more and more information concerning the maternal side of the family, the Carters of witch-haunted Arkham. His interest in family history transformed into an obsession, until at last he relocated to Arkham and became immersed in its alchemy; and the fever of his interest entered into the brains of his children, and their children. Your family is secretive by nature, and prefers to isolate itself from other Arkham residents. You yourself were tutored privately, at home, and thus escaped the lure of the cultic sect that has long infiltrated the campus of Miskatonic University."

The fellow regarded her with a curious expression playing on his features. "You have proved a dilemma to your family, Aspinwall. From an early age you have been—what does the family term it?— hyper-sensitive. You have hidden from the world and spent most of your hours studying by feeble lamplight in the huge attic of your fa-ther's home. Your refusal—or inability—to converse with others in the household was frowned upon, but nothing your father did proved a tonic to your antisocial ways. Interestingly, the one time you actually talked was when you slept, and then you spoke of those things of which you dreamed—fantastic things; and sometimes when you spoke in slumber you would lift your hands and move your fin-gers queerly, and as you did so some aspects of shadow in the attic would form themselves outlandishly, and sometimes horribly. It was this that motivated your father to send you to the notorious Edith Gnome, who had earned a wide reputation for understanding those souls who suffered from outlandish alchemical manifestation. The Gnome hag intuited that your magick had its source in your ability to connect with the world of dream, and thus she has sent you here, pretending that she needs you to assist her in finding some key of darkness. In reality, she has sent you here to find yourself."

"How wonderful that you understand everything, Simon."

"It is advantageous, when I am saddled with an extremely young creature who, although she wears an aspect of maturity, is utterly uncomprehending of everything around her. But I sense possibilities in you. You have a taint of Carter witch−blood in you, after all."

"Little good that will do me here," Agnes replied. "I doubt we can make magick serve us in this realm."

"*Au contraire,* little one. I am a sorcerer no matter where I find myself." She watched as Simon raised his eyes to the scarlet moon, as he lifted one large hand to that distant sphere and made to it an elder sign. From somewhere deep beneath them came a sound of low and mournful moaning, and Agnes noticed that the small slips of paper that littered the expanse of ground began to tremble with slight movement. Suddenly, a burst of unnatural wind broke free from be−neath the sod of dreamland, and the thousands of paper slips rose with that daemon−wind toward the moon. Agnes adjusted her eye−glasses, which had slipped a little down her nose, and watched as the slips turned crimson, burst into flame, and then extinguished as shiny obsidian cinders that littered the dreamland sky, like stars of dark ash.

The wind that had been summoned pushed at them, and Agnes, not resisting, began to move forward toward the low hills; but when she turned to look at Simon and saw that he was not following her, she stopped. "You look so disappointed, beast."

The fellow shrugged. "I will tell you a secret. I have, for the longest time, felt a keen ache to enter the dreamworld. Perhaps I wanted it so because I knew that it was absurdly denied me. And why was that denial evoked? Because I had grown too intimate with the language and the thaumaturgy of the *Necronomicon*. How pu−erile! Anyone who has studied Alhazred knows that the arcane knowledge he scribbled into his black book came to him from dreams! To master that knowledge *should* act as key *into* any realm of dream. And yet I am called 'corrupt' and denied what should so obviously be mine. I am unaccustomed to such denial. I *insist* on claiming whatever I wish mine.

"I thought there was more to this denial, that it was somehow rooted to the fact that I did not dream. I have no need of sleep, and my brain is a thing of constant activity. It does not surrender itself to slumber. That was a part of my error in thinking—associating dream with sleep. The Gnome hag assisted me, although she dislikes me keenly, and taught me the art of dreaming. She has now enabled me to enter at least this portion of the dreamworld, this dreamland of witchery. So here I am—yet this existence feels too similar to mortality as I have experienced it. I was expecting—*more*." He scanned the hills before them and tried to sense the things they may conceal. "We will find the fantastic things of this dreamland of witchery—or we will conjure the outré ourselves. Those hills await us. Come, follow me."

CHAPTER V

The conservation lab occupied a series of non–public rooms on the ground floor of the Orne Library. It was a quiet, secluded spot, with usually no one present other than Mandy or another intern. If she needed help with a procedure or had a question about the appropriate materials to use for some restoration project, Professor Ashley was generally nearby, either in the stacks or in his office. Mandy spent her weekday mornings in the lab, doing whatever conservation tasks Ashley had assigned her; and if she finished up a project before he had given her another, there was always a cartload of run–of–the–mill books waiting for simple, routine repairs that could be easily performed by an intern. As a rule, outsiders seldom ventured into the lab—it was considered off–limits by the other library staff, possibly due to the constant odor of drying glues, rotting leather bindings, musty papers, and chemical baths. If librarians needed to speak with a conservator, they would summon Ashley or one of his interns to their own office, which invariably smelled better. Which was why Mandy was surprised to look up from a page she was mending in an eighteenth–century volume to see Penelope Armitage approaching with a large parcel wrapped in dingy–looking linen tucked under her arm.

"Hello, Miss Armitage, what brings you in here today?" said the younger woman, rinsing her paste brush by swishing it around briskly in a tin can of water.

"Oh, please call me Penelope. No need to be formal, my dear. We're all family here. It's bookish types like us versus the world—

27

right? May I?" she inquired, gesturing that she wished to lay her parcel on Mandy's work table.

"Certainly. Let me clear a space for you." Mandy gingerly moved aside the antique book she had been working on, along with a paste pot and numerous strips of handmade paper that would blend in with the paper used in the book. "There you go. What have we here?"

"This monstrosity," said Penelope melodramatically, "is a vintage scrapbook from the Pascal Archive."

"You've been cataloging that collection, haven't you?" Mandy was proud of herself for knowing that obscure bit of information.

"Well, not quite cataloging it yet. I'm preparing a preliminary finding aid. Fully cataloging the Pascal Archive will take some time. At any rate, this unfortunate scrapbook and its contents are in severe need of restoration. It's a perfect mess. Some idiot has spilled a dark liquid on the thing, and half the pages are soaked in the stuff. The papers in the front—press clippings from Rebecca Pascal's early days on the stage before her film career, theater programs, that sort of thing—have mostly escaped damage, but the second half of the book, which contains photos from the 1920s and '30s, is almost entirely saturated with whatever it is. That's bad enough, but many of those back pages are also stuck together, and the photos are in danger of becoming damaged. I'm afraid the whole thing needs to be taken apart and thoroughly cleaned, if possible. Is there anything you can do to save it—to remove the gunk and make the thing usable again? I wouldn't dare put it in a patron's hands in this condition."

"Let's see," said Mandy, reaching out for the parcel. As Penelope unwound the linen wrapping and handed her the scrapbook, Mandy noticed the offending liquid had even stained the covers, although someone had managed to wipe some of the excess away. She flinched with revulsion as she took the package from the older woman. "This will definitely be a rubber gloves operation," Mandy added, half joking.

"I'd say toss the whole thing in the incinerator if the photos weren't so important. Most of the paper items can be found in other collections, but the photos are probably unique. They document not only Rebecca's professional life but also her personal life. Invaluable to an biographer, I'd say. Those are worth preserving."

"Definitely."

"Rebecca Pascal was a very famous film star in her day—long before your time, dear—and now there's a great deal of interest in her career, especially since that nasty business up at the Old Wooded Graveyard on Hangman's Hill."

Mandy's expression revealed that she had no idea what Penelope was talking about. "You know, when those occultists died in that horrible foolishness at Rebecca's tomb? It was plastered all over the *Advertiser*—surely you must have seen it."

"Oh, yes—*that*. I do remember reading about the accident. Two, or was it three of them, falling to their deaths from the roof of her mausoleum. What a tragedy."

"The only tragedy was that the authorities allow lunatics like that to run loose in Arkham!"

Mandy smirked at the intensity of Penelope's disapproval, but let it pass without comment. Instead, she turned the scrapbook this way and that, observing the extent of the staining. "What do you think this stuff is—mud or paint? It's kind of a reddish-brown, like dried blood. What on earth caused this?"

"I have no idea, dear. To tell the truth, I hadn't even noticed the scrapbook until quite recently. It was buried deep in a box of Pascal family papers that I brought home a few days ago to examine. Well, despite the best of intentions, I didn't get through the entire box and didn't find the scrapbook until the very morning that I returned it all. I was packing the car and suddenly saw this atrocity sticking up out of the box at a funny angle, as if someone had just shoved it in there. And the odd thing was, I'd had a ridiculous dream the night before, in which I'd found an old scrapbook just like this one that was soaked in blood, of all things! In the dream the scrapbook seemed like some kind of shocking evidence from a sordid crime scene—and who knows, maybe it is!"

"Weird. Well, whatever this yucky stuff is, Professor Ashley will know how to get rid of it. There's not a stain known to mankind that he can't remove."

"Wonderful. Thank you so much, dear. Please send it over when it's done."

"Sure, but don't hold your breath. It'll take me a while. By the way, what are the photos of?"

"Oh, publicity stills, location shots from her film days, portraits of friends and family, actors and actresses she worked with, stage productions, social events—that sort of thing. Nothing special, it seems, although I haven't looked at them all yet. I only examined the first few pages toward the back, before the really bad staining starts. This is just one of about a hundred scrapbooks and photo albums we received from the estate, plus there are boxes and boxes of loose press clippings, theater programs, publicity materials, and photo prints, as well as countless negatives. Rebecca was quite the amateur photographer. She loved being behind the camera lens, as well as in front of it. Richard—her great−nephew—said he kept only a dozen or so iconic images of Rebecca for a biography he talks about writing. And that's what it is: all talk. He gave the rest of the photographs to the library. There are some nice ones in there, I'll say that much. She was an uncommonly beautiful woman. But you know what they say about beauty being only skin−deep. Her heart was another matter entirely."

Chapter VI

Simon and Agnes walked to the nearest of the dark hills; and as they began to climb that lofty hill the sky above them shifted slowly in hue and became deep orange spotted with crimson clouds. A stench was carried to them on the wind that drifted from the heights, and as they approached the apex of the hill Agnes detected a queer sound that resembled the creaking of tall trees bending in a gale. The uneven surface of the hill spread before them, and Simon approached the nearest of the numerous gallows from which cadavers hung on lengths of rope.

"A veritable Gallows Hill, wouldn't you say? Observe this fellow's costume: it is of the early American era, perhaps the late seventeenth century. Well, these dreamlands must have some kind of fowl, judging from this gentleman's missing eyes. Gah, this effluvium is unpleasant."

He turned to grimace at Agnes and saw that she did not heed him, that her attention had been caught by something in the distance. Turning to ascertain what she was staring at, Simon noted the place where seven mammoth pillars formed a circle; and he detected that something, some human form, moved at the center of that circle. Agnes started to move away from him, toward the pillars, but Simon reached out for her and clutched her arm.

"We must use caution in this realm of alchemic dream. I have, since the Gnome hag spirited us to this land, sensed a kind of foreboding that I find both delicious and dangerous. I delight in vanquishing any kind of peril that may threaten me—but here, in this unholy habitat, I think I'll have to develop new skills of conquest."

Agnes did not look at him as she said, "From what I have heard of your nature, you've never been one to 'play it safe.' It's useless to try and act with caution in a land of dream. I'm ready for any kind of surprise."

"You will follow my counsel, Aspinwall."

Agnes, grinning, turned to the beast. "You insist on having your way, don't you? That's the one thing that drives you to distraction—not being in control. It'll be amusing watching you fail in mastering the situation here. You're as vulnerable as I am." So saying, she tugged her arm out of Simon's hold and marched away from him, toward the pillars and the being that moved inside their formation. Above her, the hanged figures swaying from their gallows formed weird moving shadows on the ground, and each time she stepped onto one of those shadows Agnes experienced an icy chill that seemed to seize her soul. Glancing upward as she neared the stout stone pillars, she noted the nearby gallows that was unoccupied, its vacant noose tossing in the rising gale. Passing beneath it, Agnes leaned against one of the stone pillars and watched the woman who bent over what looked like a pool of tar, which she stirred with a weighty staff. Agnes was quite frankly amazed at the woman's attire, the long and elaborate metallic dress that was perhaps constructed from silver lamé, low–cut at the woman's bosom and with a wide fabric of belt that squeezed the figure's willowy waist. Suddenly the woman began to vocalize a haunting tune, a song of such melan–choly that Agnes felt tears form in her eyes. The woman moaned her tune as her staff churned the thick black liquid of the pool, and then she stepped away from the pool as a shape began to rise from it, an ebony form that lifted itself out of the pool and onto the ground of dreamland. The tar with which this new creature was covered slipped from its nude frame as daemonic wind howled all around the scene.

"Name thy accuser!" shouted the woman in the metallic gown.

The young creature who had emerged from the pool began to struggle to speak, as if language were a thing she had not uttered for a century or more. Finally she croaked, "I name John Hale, of Mas–

sachusetts."

The other woman nodded. "Yes. But know that he repented of his murderous actions and fought to end the trials."

"Of what good was that to me, when he worked to see me swing? I was innocent, accused by one who used me carnally and then fretted for his reputation. I name John Hale."

"Very well. Touch my staff as I point it to yon post." The beautifully attired creature raised the end of her staff to the gallows that was vacant of occupant. Agnes watched as a dim shadow formed near the noose, a shadow that gradually took the form of a dead man. "His eidolon will hang there for all of dreamland eternity. Go now, and roam this realm that is your eternal haunt." The nude woman bowed to the other and stepped out of the circle of antique pillars. Agnes felt her flesh chill as the other woman turned to regard her.

Suddenly, Simon stepped past Agnes and approached the tall woman, who grasped her staff protectively. "How can you be here?" he shouted. "You have been dead these many years!"

"Are the dead not allowed to dream, Simon Williams? The curious thing is that you have entered this spectral land, for you have also insisted that you do not dream."

"Why the devil are you so tall? I remember you being rather short in reality."

"One of the wonderful qualities in dreamland is that we can change aspects of our physical nature. I have made some few alterations. I advise you to try—your face has always been a product of horror for the unfortunate souls who have looked upon it."

Agnes almost wanted to laugh at how flustered the beast of Sesqua Valley seemed in the presence of the other woman, but she did her best not to smile as he turned his bewildered eyes to her. "Aspinwall, I introduce you to Rebecca Pascal, incarnated here as she was at the height of her film career. I knew her later in her life, when she was the center of an occult conclave in detestable Arkham."

Rebecca smiled and nodded to Agnes, and then she looked at

Simon again. "You have always hated Arkham because it was one place where you held no authority, where you could not control the alchemy of that depraved witch—town. And now you have entered the dreamland of witches, where you will find yourself equally lack—ing in clout. How amusing."

Agnes turned and looked at the countless gallows of the area. "Who are these men?"

Rebecca walked beyond them, out of the circle of pillars and to the post from which the newest corpse swung. "They are the men who murdered witches in eras past. Unlike their victims, they were corrupt and guilty. Thus we beckon them here to make them suffer for their crimes." She turned to Agnes and held out her hand, and the younger woman moved toward her. "Unlike you," Rebecca continued, "the women accused were vacant of witchery—in most cases, at any rate. But you are the authentic thing, young as you are. What brings your dreaming self to this realm?"

"I was sent here on a mission for a friend. I seek a key of dark—ness and death. I confess to feeling a bit out of my depths. I don't know where to start. But I have Simon here to assist me in my quest."

Rebecca Pascal shrugged. "Well, he will at least prove an enter—tainment; but I doubt he will have much assistance to offer you. No, don't frown. You have found me, and I will aid thee in thy expedi—tion."

Chapter VII

Once she had the scrapbook disbound, Mandy began removing the paper ephemera and photographs from various pages so she could treat the stains. She did this using a warm, damp cloth poultice pressed against the back side of the page. Then she placed each page and its poultice under a weight and set it aside. In a day or two, the moisture in the poultice would soften the adhesive; at that point, some items would come loose from the page on their own. Others were more stubborn; on these she used a small spatula, gingerly probing at the joint of the item to the page until she was able to peel it carefully away. It was delicate work, but she enjoyed it, and the days spent doing this task went by quickly. Once the stained paper items—clippings and such—were detached, she tested them to see if they would hold up to being exposed to water. Given the acidic wood pulp used in the manufacture of most papers in the early twentieth century, it was a roll of the dice immersing them in a bath, but none of them showed any signs of damage during the tests, so she proceeded to minimize and in some cases entirely remove the stains by soaking the items and their mounting pages in trays of distilled water and then gently cleaning them with a soft brush. Then she laid them between sheets of blotter paper to dry.

In cases where pages with photos were stuck together, it was a twostage process. First she used a poultice to separate the pages, and then another poultice on the back sides of the photos to unstick them. The trick was not to cause any peeling of the photographic emulsion; that would ruin the image. This part made her nervous, but it went smoothly. As the photos were separated, she placed them into trays of water. They looked so much better as the blood residue—or whatever it was—gradually ebbed away into the bath, revealing the clean images.

It was on the fourth day of this process that Mandy discovered the photographs of monsters. That's what she called them: real effing monsters. Not kids in creepy Halloween customs. Not rubber—suited actors from some hokey B—grade horror movie. These were actual fiends, demonic entities captured in mid—flight as they flitted past Rebecca Pascal's windows on moonlit nights. She didn't see the bizarre images until she had pulled apart two pages that were practically glued together. Until that moment, the strange and disturbing photos had been concealed, hidden between the pages. There were five images in all, and they would be worth a lot of money to the right buyer. Best of all, Penelope didn't even know they existed. Which meant she would never miss them. Mandy's heart began to beat wildly and she caught herself hyperventilating as she slipped the still damp pictures into a small envelope and tucked it into the waistband of her black skirt, under her blouse.

Deciding it was time for a break, she grabbed her cigarettes and lighter from her purse and quickly strode to the rear of the lab where levered windows in metal frames extended the length of the back wall. She unlatched a window and tilted it down into the open position, then lit a cigarette and blew a long hissing stream of smoke through the gap between window and frame. Mandy loved this spot. It was the only place at work where she could smoke without having to pass through security to leave the building. And it was a very good place for slipping stuff like small, rare, uncatalogued books out the window and into the bushes where she could pick them up later after the library had closed. Looking around to make sure she wasn't being observed, Mandy pulled the packet of monster photos from where she had concealed it in her attire, lifted it to the open window, and let it fall with a light thud into the neatly trimmed hedge below. It was like dropping an envelope full of cash into the night deposit box at her bank. *Ka—Ching!*

Chapter VIII

The late afternoon sun made for long shadows in Arkham's Chinatown. Knowing it was almost impossible to find a parking spot on the crowded streets, Mandy parked on the southern edge of the bustling district and walked the four blocks in to the Red Dragon Antique Shop. A text message from the proprietor, a certain "Dr. Lang"—she didn't know his first name—had expressed keen interest in the items she was offering. Like many establishments in the area, it was a long, narrow space crowded with far too much bizarre junk. The lighting was barely adequate and the air was stuffy, as if the entire place needed a good cleaning. Dr. Lang most likely would be in the back of the shop, at the counter, fussing with his silly packages. A bell had jingled when she opened the front door and he had called out "Hello! Be right with you!"

"Hi, Dr. Lang. Stay there; I'll come to you." She rounded a corner where a large teak armoire protruded into the aisle and saw him at his post, opening a cardboard shipping container with a box knife.

"Oh, it's *you*," he said in a tone that was distinctly disrespectful.

"Yes, it's me. Your friendly supplier."

"The little girl thief who tries to sell me her hot merchandise. What do you think I am—a fence? This is not some shady downtown pawnshop. I've got a respectable business to run here."

She gave him a *Really? You're going there?* look.

"You said you wanted to see these new arrivals, Dr. Lang."

"Maybe I changed my mind. The stuff you bring me has no provenance. I could get in a lot of trouble."

"Dr. Lang, I wouldn't have bothered coming all the way down here had I known you have doubts about the legitimacy of my wares. I only deal in authentic vintage collectibles acquired from—"

"Stolen from that library you work at! I'm no dummy; I didn't fall off the turnip truck yesterday."

"—acquired from the finest sources. Now listen: do you want to see them or not?"

Lang frowned, staring deep into her eyes. His long, black eye—brows—twisted and tangled at the ends—made him look even more ferocious than he really was.

"I can take these elsewhere. There are other buyers for rarities like these. You think you're the only one with an interest in the oc—cult?" She turned as if she were about to leave.

"No, wait a minute. Show me what you have."

Mandy's face lit up, and she opened her purse and removed a small rectangular object wrapped in a black silk scarf. "That's more like it!" she said, smiling broadly. She unwound the scarf to reveal a small, very old book bound in light brown calf leather. The front and back boards were decorated with a band of gold—tooled mystical symbols that had been stamped around the edges. Mandy carefully opened the volume to show him its title page, upon which in a heavy Gothic typeface were the words "El Susurro de las Avispas."

"Ah . . ." sighed Dr. Lang, now keenly intrigued. "The Spanish translation of *The Whispering of the Wasps.* I've heard of this edi—tion but never seen one. Reputed to be a most powerful grimoire."

"Printed in Madrid in the year 1758," said Mandy with feigned drama, handing him the book with both covers supported, one in each palm.

"The condition is rough. These hinges are weak."

"But it's complete. Many copies are lacking the title page. Owners would often tear it out, fearing the local church authorities would discover they owned such a blasphemous tract. A lot of copies also have the title obliterated on the spine. This one has a clear, readable title, with the gold lettering still bright. You just don't find them like this. Not this nice."

"I suppose," said Lang in a fake tone of boredom, pretending to be less desirous of the sinister volume than he actually was. "What do you want for it?"

"A thousand."

Lang burst into derisive laughter. "Ridiculous! I won't pay a penny over three hundred!"

"That's way too low, and you know it," argued Mandy. "I'd be willing to let it go for seven hundred and fifty dollars."

"Five hundred," said Lang, handing the book back to her and then folding his arms defiantly across his chest. "Take it or leave it."

Long before this meeting, Mandy had decided she would accept two hundred for the book if Lang was being a tight−ass. Five hun− dred sounded good to her, but she didn't let him know that. Instead, she went through the faux motions of hemming and hawing, weighing the offer in her mind.

Finally she said, "Okay. Five hundred. I can do that."

Lang smiled victoriously. "Very good. And the other item, the set of photographs. You have those with you?"

"I do." Mandy took an envelope from her purse and removed five vintage snapshots from it, laying them on the counter as if she were showing a winning poker hand. "Read 'em and weep."

Lang's eyes bugged out in disbelief, and he leaned closer to the images and studied each one in turn. A few he flipped over to ex− amine the back.

"These are authentic—you're sure of it?"

"Completely. They are estate−fresh from an impeccable source. I guarantee their authenticity. Your money back if they turn out to be fake."

Lang was clearly stunned by the black−and−white photos of what he recognized were night−gaunts. He wagged his head from side to side, barely able to accept the reality of what he was seeing.

"When were these taken?" he asked, looking up at her with new respect.

"A handwritten caption on the album page they were mounted on says 1931. That's probably reliable. You know these were taken by the silent film star Rebecca Pascal, don't you? She died a few years ago, and these were found among her effects."

"I figured as much. She is rumored to have had multiple en−counters with night−gaunts over the course of her life. I had heard there might be some photos but never expected any to turn up. These are remarkable."

Mandy picked up one of the photos and studied it. The creatures were as large as a man and looked vaguely human, except they had wings like bats and their bodies were as scrawny as Holocaust survi−vors. She looked closer and noticed again something that had really creeped her out when she first examined the images: the creatures had no faces. Where there should have been eyes, a nose, a mouth, was only a smooth, featureless polyp of flesh.

"Ugly suckers," she muttered.

"Hmm?" said Lang.

"Oh, nothing. So are you interested?" She knew he was, pas−sionately so.

Dr. Lang didn't even try to conceal his enthusiasm. "I am. Very much. What's your asking price?"

"Two thousand, and that's firm. I walk out of here with these and you'll never see them again. I promise you that much."

Lang didn't look up to test her resolve. He couldn't take his eyes off the shocking images. In a sudden sweeping gesture he scooped all five snapshots up and placed them in the envelope that Mandy had left on the counter.

"Okay," he said matter−of−factly. "Deal."

"It's a deal, then."

Lang opened the cash register and took out a thick wad of twenties. "Twenty−five hundred total," he said, counting out bills. Seeing the stack of money he was handing her, Mandy felt a tre−mendous rush throughout her body, as if she were in love, or in heaven. She couldn't quit smiling. She knew that for future bargain−ing advantage she should play it cool, as if it were no big deal, but she was too damned thrilled to hide her satisfaction. That good feel−ing lasted all afternoon and on into the evening.

Chapter IX

Rebecca led them over the seven hills of dreamland; and when, at last, they reached the apex of the seventh hill and looked at the antique town below them, Agnes gasped in joy.

"It's exactly as Manly described it," she informed them as she moved a little away from the group.

"Whatever are you muttering about, Aspinwall?" Simon queried, a sour expression twisting his features.

Agnes turned to the beast, her eyes wide with wonder. "Come on, Simon, you've read William Davis Manly. Don't you remember his prose-poem sequence, 'Witch-Town,' in which he evoked a kind of fairytale image of a place inhabited by alchemists and sorcerers? Manly's language as a prose-poet was keenly influenced by Clark Ashton Smith, and he delighted in expressing dark things in gorgeous imagery. I've read his small book of prose-poems so many times that I have most of it memorized—and now I see it before me.

> "'It was a thing that dwelt beyond the dark threshold of midnight dreaming, and its habitations were of such an age that they might have existed always, a town grown out of the hoary ground, composed of structures that owned a kind of uncanny sentience. Above the town, the sky was murky, bereft on starlight or moongleam; as if such radiance would mar the sorcery of the place and the things that abided within it.'"

Rebecca listened to the younger woman's recitation, not smiling. "I find that I disagree with your poet. Moonlight, if it's ghastly

41

enough, can aid the alchemy of an ancient setting." She lifted her eyes to the black sky and began to whisper so softly that the others could not make out her words; but they were able to witness its effect, as high above them a small dot of white light began to expand in size, until it formed a sphere that aped the moon of the waking world. The pale beams that fell onto the olden town revealed its crooked shadows and were reflected on the creeks and tributaries, the broken spire of an abandoned church, and the hunched figures that crept along the byways.

"Now, confess, Miss Aspinwall," Rebecca said, "is that not enchanting?"

"Please, call me Agnes. Yes, it does have its own charm; but I think I prefer utter darkness, and its secrets."

Simon sniffed derisively. "That's because you prefer to hide yourself away from the world and keep your secrets to yourself. You cannot comprehend the joy that comes from divulging those things within us, however outlandish or confusing one may find them." He turned to Rebecca. "Speaking of which, you have yet to explain your presence here. I have heard the story of your final destruction—of how your soul was utterly desiccated and flung into the Outside void, or some such thing. How is it that you exist in dreamland?"

The elder woman turned to him with a pitying look. "For one who is rumored to have memorized the *Necronomicon,* you are woefully ignorant. Do you not remember what Alhazred has written of dreaming, and of extending the very core of one's being into dream-life? It takes great skill and fortitude, I admit—and I had both, in abundance. When I realized that I faced mortal extinction, I entered a mode of deepest dreaming, in which I projected the core of my personality, that immaterial essence which exists beyond or outside our mortal clay. Perhaps you cannot understand this because you are not human but immortal, a thing composed of Sesqua Valley's mist and shadow. My sorcery was a potent force, Simon, one that did not languish when I died, when my soul was cast to the Outer One known as Kamog. I no longer exist, in any fashion, in the waking world. Here, in the dreamlands, I cannot be touched."

Their conversation ended abruptly when they noticed that their young acquaintance was no longer with them but halfway down the seventh hill, stumbling toward the moonlit witch—town with an ex— pression of wonder on her countenance. They followed her down the hill, as Simon reached into his jacket's inner pocket and pro— duced a lean red flute. As he began to play music, even he was astonished at how the melody was transmogrified by the aether of dreamland, which took his song and warped it bizarrely. Simon breathed his song, and he smelled the wind that began to rise as if in answer to his melody, the warm wind that encased his face and whispered at his large ears.

Agnes heard the rising wind inside the hollows of her ears, and it amazed her that wind could be so articulate. She sensed, beneath the moan of nature, other echoes of whispered words and chants and summoning; as if an entire populace of this witch—town were repre— sented on the rushing gust, a choral of rising tempest that greeted her to the enchanted realm. She raised her eyes to the moon and watched the clouds that, now and then, passed near it; and she noted the weird outline many of those clouds presented, as if they were the shadows of formless things that, expanding and contracting, struggle to represent some solid figure. Lowering her gaze, Agnes watched the moonlit shadows of the moving clouds on the dirt road before her, and she began to whistle to the tune of Simon's flute as she fol— lowed the crawling shadows, past the hovels and slanting walls of taller buildings, into an open district where stood a large fountain composed of red stone. Sitting at the fountain's apex was a shrouded genderless thing, at the sight of which Simon's music ceased. They listened to the other sound that issued from the sky above them and seemed to pulse within two low—hanging crimson clouds—the beating of primordial drums; and as they listened to the pounding reverberation from the sky they smelled the sulfurous stench that leaked from those crimson clouds and tainted the night air.

Simon stepped nearer to the fountain and bowed to the lumpish figure that squatted at the fountain's zenith. Straightening, he took in the robe of yellow silk figured with zigzag lines of red and the mask of yellow silk that enshrouded the figure's face.

"We come, High-Priest, in search of the Key of Blackness, which is rumored to unlock the mysteries of the Worm."

An awful voice responded: "That will be found within the top-most cavern of K'nath, the twin-peak daemon of ebony stone that broods over this witch-town. It is now concealed by the smoke of midnight—but I can conjure its contour."

Simon bowed a second time and made certain signs with one hand; and then the little group watched as the lurker atop the fountain fumbled at its lap and produced a macabre carven flute of ivory, which it raised to its mask-enshrouded mouth. The wretched music emitted from the monster's flute was a lunatic variation of the melody that Simon had performed, and as its sound coiled around the listeners the reek from the crimson clouds intensified. The dreamworld's loathsome high-priest raised a mammoth slippered foot that pointed to a distant place beyond the huddled roofs of witch-town, and a pall of blackness seemed to part, revealing a part of sky that wore the lighter shade of twilight—and in that twilight stood a mammoth twin-peaked mountain of ebony rock that resembled some slumbering daemon. Simon gazed at the titan of stone for many moments, and then he returned his flute to his mouth and began to play.

CHAPTER X

Penelope hadn't meant to nap, and certainly hadn't planned on fall—ing into a deep slumber while sitting comfortably in the shade with her back resting against an ancient oak in the center of a high pasture tucked into the hills behind Arkham. The isolated pasture was one of her favorite places, a treasured secret that she shared with no one. She came there often after work, bringing a thermos of hot tea and a book. No matter how stressful or simply dull her day had been, something about this setting placed her mind at ease again. Perhaps it was the rich, fecund scent of the abundant wildflowers growing all around, or perhaps the refreshing breeze that swept in from the sea smelling of starfish and sunken galleys. Maybe it was merely the cap—tivating view of Arkham spread out below her, a complex mass of gambrel roofs and white church spires whose streets held countless stories that she would never know. Whatever the reason, it was a place of solace for her—indeed, it was balm for her spirit.

Her father had taught her of this place, bringing her here for picnic lunches when she was a small child. He said it was a very spe—cial place, known only to the fairies—a place where magic could happen. As if to prove his point, he would show her the many fairy rings that bloomed across the pasture during the damp autumn days, but he always warned her not to step inside the circles of fungi, for if she did, the fairies might carry her away to their fey land beyond time.

Once Penelope had reached the age of reason, she stopped be—lieving these fanciful tales of fairies and magical circles, and yet the high pasture still remained a charmed place in her imagination.

The book she had brought this time was a work of nonfiction: a brief history of the witchcraft trials of 1692. She didn't believe in witch-craft per se, as evidence of the paranormal; it was all balderdash and hys-teria as far as she was concerned, but the subject kept coming up in her work at the reference desk at Orne Library. More and more, students were requesting research materials relating to witchcraft, or bluntly asking her their questions on the topic, and she invariably felt ill-equipped to aid them properly. A brushing up on the little she had learned about the witchcraft trials in her college history class was in order. She poured herself a steaming cup of black tea, took a bol-stering sip, and began reading. Not three pages in, she drifted off into a woozy unconsciousness.

Her dream was most unusual. While she was dreaming she knew that she was doing so, but that fact did not make her awaken with a start as it normally would have. Furthermore, the dream had a most uncanny feel to it, one she had experienced only once before, in a long, elaborate dream that had come to her a few weeks before. As in that mystifying dream, she was in a strange landscape, one both supernatural and melancholy. It didn't feel like any version of the everyday world that she lived in. It was a place unto itself, with its own undeniable sense of reality. Unsure just how to conduct herself in this visionary realm, she took it as it came—on its terms, and not hers.

"I could scream or shake myself awake, but something tells me not to do that. I need to experience this, whatever it is, to receive the lesson that has been prepared for me."

She had been walking through a haunted wood, alone, for an indeterminate time. Leaving behind the dense vegetation, she found herself within a large, subterranean complex of caverns and hollowed out chambers that seemed to be a vast church-like structure situated deep within the rocky crust of whatever planet she was on. The par-ticular room she was in had a name; it was "The Hall of Remem-brance." Somehow she knew this, although no one had told her. She was not alone there. Three tall, feminine bird-like beings who

identified themselves only as "The Rememberers" were in the process of verbally examining her, asking a series of probing, emotion-
laden questions. Each question was more terrible than the last in the
way it penetrated her psyche and made her feel sad and unworthy.
The questions were supposed to be rhetorical—that's what they had
told her at the start, anyway—and yet she felt compelled to answer
them as honestly as she could. The final question thoroughly devas-
tated Penelope, bringing back long-buried memories of a difficult
period during her senior year of high school when she had been in
love with a young man—a boy really—and it hadn't worked out.
Her family had forced her to break off the relationship with him, to
end it coldly, for what she felt—then and now—were unwarranted
reasons. He had been raised in the wrong religion, as a Jew, and he
was "not our kind," according to her mother.

The three Rememberers chanted in eerie unison with singsong
voices that blended into one damning song:

"What would your children look like, had you married?
Boys or girls, or one of each?
How would they number, and would you cherish them?
Would they fill up your heart?"

As if it were not enough that these heinous harpies were mania-
cally screeching at Penelope, at the same time they flapped their long
arms wildly about, causing their heavy white satin robes adorned
with iridescent white feathers to flap up and down in cruel mockery
of her.

At that point Penelope had broken down entirely, collapsing into
grief as she wept profusely, her tears splashing into a stone basin
where they swirled round and round while withered rose petals
ebbed in the eddies. This basin was mounted on a large stone table at
which Penelope was seated, across from the standing Rememberers.
She noticed a drain at the bottom of it, down which her tears had
coursed. The Rememberers impassively watched without offering
any consolation.

Finally composing herself enough to speak, she sobbed, "Where do they go, my tears?" The Remembers again sang in a single unified voice as they madly thrashed their wing—like robes:

"They disappear downward and are carried away
Through pipes to be mixed with the tears of others,
Mortals like yourself, oh foolish sufferers,
Bound for the Great Well of Sorrow,
Known to your race as the Fount of Tears.
But of this truth, we will say no more,
And you'll not retain memory of this ceremony."

And with that, Penelope suddenly woke up under the tree, the book splayed open on the grass beside her, her tea spilled and soaking into the black soil. Sunset was rapidly approaching, reddening the eastern clouds. She didn't want to be caught there after dark, so she rose up hastily, brushed the leaves from her dress, gathered her things together, pulled on a sweater she had brought along, and started the walk for home.

CHAPTER XI

Mandy Peaslee's table was well situated in a brightly lit corner of the front dining area at the Hobo Bean Coffee Company, a popular downtown hangout for the students and faculty of nearby Miskatonic University. She was just finishing up her lunch, a Caesar salad, pushing the unwanted bits of chicken around on the plate with her fork, when she spotted the creepy graduate student sitting two tables over, against the wall below a large framed vintage Mexican movie poster. The poster was for a film called *Demonio del Sol,* and its crudely painted artwork depicted a woman in a pink nightgown with pointy breasts being devoured by a giant green–faced fiend that appeared to be half–man, half–beast.

Demon Sun, Mandy thought, guessing at a translation. She had forgotten most of the Spanish she had learned in high school. Or, perhaps it meant *Demon of My Soul.* But *Sol* meant "Sun," didn't it? It had to be *Demon Sun.*

He was a boyish–looking kid with blond hair and a pasty complexion. She didn't know his name and didn't want to know it. She suspected he had a schoolboy crush on her; he was always "accidentally" running into her in the library stacks and starting ridiculous conversations. It was on his recommendation that she had borrowed a book of poems by some old hag named Edith Gnome from the library, had taken it home to read one night, and as a result had strange dreams. He was always jabbering away about "the occult." She wasn't sure if he had a genuine interest in the subject, if he was obsessed about it like Dr. Lang, or if he feigned an interest as a way of—so he imagined—making points with her. Maybe he thought it made him sound like an intellectual, a deep thinker. Which was a crock. Most of these "occultists" at M.U. were freaking idiots—and the place was crawling with them. "Throw a rock at Miskatonic and you'll hit an occultist!" went the saying, and it was true.

Oh God, she thought, *He's coming over here.*

"Hi, Mandy. Mind if I join you?"

Somehow he knew her name. That was stalker-ish of him. Before she had time to answer, he pulled out the chair opposite her and plunked himself down in it.

"Sure. There's plenty of room."

He had brought his coffee with him and now was going through exaggerated motions of warming his hands on the waxed paper cup, as if it were the dead of winter and the hot coffee the room's only heat source.

"How'd you like the Edith Gnome book?" he asked.

"Oh, very interesting. Thanks for recommending it."

"She was a notorious witch of Arkham, you know. A true practitioner of the craft. In the seventeenth century they would have hanged her, but seeing as she lived in the twentieth century, nobody paid much attention to her casting of spells and such."

"No, I don't suppose they would have."

He leaned in conspiratorially, and his voice dropped to a whisper. "Say, I heard an interesting rumor. I heard you sold some rare photographs of night-gaunts to a local businessman. In fact, they're not just rare, they're unique: the only known photos of night-gaunts is what I heard."

"That's not true. Where would I get such things?"

"Well, you work in the library and have unlimited access to the materials stored there, right?"

"Hardly. I do work at the library, but my access is quite limited. I only handle materials that require conservation or repair work. And then I have access to them only when I'm actually working on them. Otherwise, I have to check things in and out just like anyone else."

"Doc Lang says you snagged the photos before they were cata—

loged and sold them to him for a tidy sum."

"He's lying. And what's it to *you*, anyway?" She was starting to sound annoyed.

"Oh, it's nothing to me. Forget I said anything. I'm just making small talk."

"I'm afraid I know nothing about such photographs. I've never even heard of them."

"Okay, I believe you, Mandy. Lang obviously made up the whole thing. That explains why he wouldn't show them to me or my associates."

"Your *associates?*" There was a note of condescension in Mandy's tone.

"Yeah. The guys I hang out with. We call ourselves 'The Smoke and Ash Society,' but we're commonly known around campus as the 'Black−Clad Occultists.'"

"A gang of troublemakers, no doubt," Mandy said sarcastically.

"Go ahead and laugh, but we take ourselves seriously, and someday everyone else will, too."

"My, my—that sounds like a terrorist threat. Maybe I should report you to the authorities."

"Maybe I should report you to the cops. Just kidding, Mandy!"

She pulled a book from her purse and flopped it open to a random page. "Well, if you'll pardon me, I have some studying to do."

"Certainly. Nice talking to you, Mandy. Let me know if you find any more pictures of night−gaunts," he said with a wink. Then he got up and left.

With the creepy grad student gone, her gaze drifted back to the *Demonio del Sol* poster on the wall above where he had sat. It reminded her of something she'd read the night before on a blog called "Haunted Arkham." Some gossip piece about the three people who had died after falling off the roof of Rebecca Pascal's tomb on the night her cult group—or were they her coven?—had swarmed the graveyard up on Hangman's Hill. One of them had been, it was claimed, Rebecca herself. Which made no sense whatsoever, because she was already long dead at that point. Supposedly this was her rot−

ting corpse, preternaturally animated by her surviving spirit. So she died a second time, if that was even possible.

The second victim was some chump named Abraham Wait. He was, it is alleged, the leader of the Black–Clad Occultists, or what did the grad student call them? The Smoke and Mirror Club? Wait was a charismatic student at Miskatonic who had, so the story goes, befriended the reanimated Rebecca and gained her confidence enough to be at her side during some weird summoning ceremony where the cultists attempted to call down from outer space an obscure alien god called "Kamog."

The third victim who died in a plunge from the roof of Rebecca's tomb was a loser named Wilus Lorne. She'd heard about him. He was, among other things, a book scout who dabbled in the occult. Lang had mentioned buying some forbidden books from him. The blogger claimed that what had actually happened to this trio was that their "souls were devoured by Kamog." Yeah, sure they were. Anyway, that's what the image on the poster looked like to Mandy: a woman having her soul eaten by a monster. The fiend's hairy face was half–green and half–purple, and its long fangs were in the process of piercing the belly and breasts of the unfortunate woman in the pink nightgown. Was he about to eat her soul?

"Well, good afternoon, Miss Peaslee." It was good old Penelope Armitage, holding before her slight figure a small cardboard tray containing half a sandwich wrapped in paper and a plastic bowl of clam chowder.

Mandy snapped out of her reverie and gave Armitage her friendliest fake smile. "How pleasant to see you, Miss Armitage. Do have a seat, if you can spare the time."

"Actually," said Penelope in her usual gravelly voice, "I'm on my way back to the office, but I can chat for a moment." She sat down delicately across from Mandy in the same chair the creepy grad student had just vacated. "Lots to do on that Pascal Archive. I'm working through lunch most days. The woman was a terrible packrat. She never threw out anything."

"That's how collections are born, right?"

"Indeed. By the way, how well do you know that young man with whom you were just conversing?" Penelope's face took on a sudden serious cast.

"Not very well, I'm afraid. I don't even know his name, although he certainly knows mine."

"Well, I do; he's Charles Morelle. He and another young fellow, a student named Abraham Wait, staged a scandalous act of larceny right before my very eyes. It was a few months ago, when I was tending the reference desk. This Morelle character acted as a human shield, blocking my view while Wait tore a page from a rare book in our collection. I didn't see the actual vandalism occur, but the sound of ripping paper was unmistakable; and sure enough, when I later examined the volume in question, there was a page missing. Because I didn't actually observe the deed being done, I was in no position to report them, but I did alert the other librarians and we've kept a close eye on these hooligans. They seem to have a special interest in the Rebecca Pascal Archive, and Morelle has barged into my office on several occasions demanding to see certain items he imagines are part of the archive. Items of an occult nature. I've sent him away empty-handed more than once."

"How odd," said Mandy, genuinely intrigued by what Penelope was telling her. "I do get a bad feeling in his presence, as if he is hiding something."

"I would be very wary of that young man if I were you, dear. He's not to be trusted. And Lord only knows what his intentions are relative to you. I sincerely doubt he is a gentleman, or that he has the proper respect for a young lady's virtue or reputation."

"Thank you for the warning, Miss Armitage—"

"Please, call me Penelope."

"Penelope."

"That's better." The older woman suddenly stood up with her tray again held out before her. "Well, duty calls. Good afternoon, dear."

"Enjoy your lunch."

Mandy's cell phone burbled, notifying her of a new text message from Dr. Lang reading "Do you have negatives or other prints? Price is no object."

She typed a reply with both thumbs in rapid fire: "I thought we had a non−disclosure agreement. Keep your mouth shut! Unknown if there are negs or prints. I'll look, but no more leaks, understood?"

Chapter XII

Rebecca was the first to notice the shifting stench on the air as they passed through and exited the witch–town, and her eyes shimmered as they beheld what looked like a rising meadow on a large incline of land beside the road they followed. Shutting her eyes and raising one elegant arm, Rebecca seemed to reach out to the aura of the mead–ow; and as the night–wind moved the folds of her fantastic gown, Agnes walked past her, off the road and onto the meadow ground, which she soon realized was a mammoth burying ground with stones as black and ancient as any found in New England.

Agnes sensed a shadow cloud her, although how there could be shadows in such a lightless place bewildered her. "Ah, sweet child," came Rebecca's mesmerizing voice, "there is but one additional thing that would give this scene completion. Hold out your hand."

The young woman did as commanded, and watched as Rebecca took a sharp black needle out of her hair and touched its point to Agnes's finger. A drop of dark blood welled from the wound, and then that petite globe of gore detached from the human hand and sailed above them, expanding into a lustrous sphere of liquid crimson hue. It floated above them, to the pale disc that was the conjured moon of white light; and as they watched, the ruddy sphere spilled its essence into the pallid disc, and a blood–drenched illumination sullied the dreamland of witchery.

Rebecca strode onto the graveyard ground and walked through its grass, which was pale milky green in color. Bending low next to one slab, she clawed into the earth and brought particles of sod to her face as she moved her lips with unspoken chanting. As if in re-sponse to her silent language, a shadow began to coil just above the ground next to the ancient stone marker. Simon, sensing rare alche-my, approached the place and sniffed, and then he knelt and began to wash his large hands in the pool of churning shadow. He gasped as that shadow lifted before him and shaped itself as a hooded figure that resembled a traditional Grim Reaper, although no semblance of bleached bone revealed itself within the figure's cowl. His silver eyes gleaming in the crimson moonlight, Simon brought his flute to his mouth and breathed an eerie tune. He was vaguely aware of the other coils of shadow that lifted in the field of death and drifted to Rebecca. The film actress reached out to the specters as they began to remove her gown, and her supple flesh drank in the ruddy moonlight as, naked, she danced beneath the crimson lunar glare. Rebecca moved her mouth again, but now her language was spoken with force, loudly and audaciously. Beams of blood-red moonlight encased her, an illumination that was worked by the sinister figures that surrounded her and woven into a tight burgundy gown.

The cowled ghosts broke apart and fell as insubstantial debris into the ground. Drifting to Simon, Rebecca removed the flute from his large mouth and pressed her lips to his. When she moved her face from his, she saw no sign of emotion on his countenance. Then he smiled faintly and, taking his flute from her grasp, walked away, re-turning to the road. "There's not an ounce of human blood coursing inside your veins," Rebecca called to him.

"No, indeed," Simon replied. "I am as inhuman as you are now, and happy to be so. Of course, this is not my physical shell, but an image spawned by dreamland magick."

"If that's so," Agnes chimed in, "how could I have bled when my finger was pricked by her black pin?"

Rebecca laughed. "Ah, the folly of trying to make sense of any-thing that occurs in dreamland! Let go of your waking world need for order and sanity. To dwell in this dreamworld is to drink fantastic madness."

"We're here on a specific mission, of which we mustn't lose sight."

Rebecca sneered and looked at Simon. "Is she always so prag‐matic?"

He shrugged. "She's young and inexperienced. But she's right—we are here to accomplish a special task, and to do so we must jour‐ney to the black mountain. How queer that our mountain in Sesqua Valley should have its varied counterparts in a variety of dreamlands. But perhaps that's not so strange, for Sesqua Valley is not quite firmly rooted in reality. If it had been, I might never have existed."

Simon turned to study his young companion's eyes, and squinted at their expression of confused worry. "What is it now, Aspinwall?"

"We're not complete."

His low laughter was a mocking sound. "What the devil is that supposed to mean?"

"There are others that are destined to join us. Can't you sense it? Our circle isn't whole."

Simon laughed again, but Rebecca held up a silencing hand. "Do not be so quick to jeer, Simon. Agnes is here on a journey of self‐discovery and alchemical growth. Her dreamland nostrils suck in the influence of sorcery with which this world is fashioned. She has budding instincts that are being stretched, intuitions that we, in our world‐weary complacency, are not tuned in to. You and I, Simon, roam this realm as seasoned necromancers, and our maturity of mag‐ick has made us proud and self‐assured, so much so that we might miss the subtle reverberations that a novice may pick up. No, we mustn't laugh or deride. We may yet have much to learn from the innocence of this witch‐child."

"I doubt that there is anything in the nature of supernatural wonder that this infant can teach me," Simon responded.

But Rebecca wasn't listening to him; for she was watching the younger woman with interested eyes, and sensed that Agnes was correct. There were others, of unknown origin, who would com‐plete their company. Stepping to Agnes, Rebecca took her hand and kissed her hair. They stood together for some moments, and then Agnes began to lead the elder women from the burying ground, down to the road that they began once more to trod.

CHAPTER XIII

It had been a bad day at work. Penelope's boss, Dr. Morgan, had asked if she had given any thought to retiring in the near future. He didn't mean anything in particular by it—he was merely making small talk—but what it said to her is that she was getting old, the years were starting to show on her, and people were expecting she would be moving on any day now. That's the way it went around there. An employee reached sixty and the countdown clock started ticking. The next thing you knew, the Sunshine Committee was throwing a potluck with gag gifts and everyone was wishing you good luck in your "new life" of sitting at home staring at the four walls.

She had no desire to retire just yet. Her work was meaningful and satisfying, and she liked being part of something larger, a group working together toward a common goal. She felt a certain pride in serving the library and the university, in being an active professional and not just another pathetic old woman fussing around her house all day, alone. And damn it, she was good at her job! Decades of experience had honed her skills and given her wisdom. Why quit now when she was in her prime? And yet, people were starting to ask: "When are you going to leave this madhouse behind and start enjoying life, Penelope?"

"Haven't given it much thought," was her stock answer, although she thought about it quite often these days. Morgan's innocent little question had ruined her morning. After lunch, thinking she was over it, she'd gone into the restroom to freshen up and had unexpectedly began sobbing. Not actually shedding tears—her self-control wasn't that far gone. Rather, a dry-eyed welling up of sadness from deep inside. Luckily, she was alone in there, with no one to witness that embarrassing moment of weakness and self-pity.

"Buck up, Missy," she had muttered to her own reflection in the mirror. "Could be worse. You have your health, and they can't force you to quit. You decide when you leave, not them. They can all go to hell."

She washed her face, dried off with paper towels, ran a brush leisurely through her hair, and returned to her desk, composure regained.

That evening, she wanted nothing more than to lose herself in a book. Immediately after dinner, she put on her nightgown and went to the bookcase looking for something unusual, something so unrelated to her everyday world that it would take her completely out of herself.

Running her index finger along a row of spines, she stopped at a slender volume she had started reading a while back and hadn't finished. It was an odd little collection of poetry by none other than the very woman whose archive she was currently indexing at work: the late film star Rebecca Pascal. The last time she had dipped into the book, she had fallen asleep and had a long, wild dream that she could barely remember upon waking. Something about finding a long-lost loved one and the joy of having him back in her life, and then suddenly losing him again and the sorrow of that. But she was foggy on the exact nature of the person in relation to her. Was it some would-be lover who existed only in dreams, or was it a cherished family member, someone she had known in real life? She just didn't recall.

Penelope pulled the book from the shelf and glanced at the title: *Step into the Moonlight and Other Poems.* Yes, that would do the trick. If it didn't put her to sleep, it would take her mind off the retirement question.

She curled up in her favorite chair, the overstuffed one she had inherited from Grandpa Henry, with her bare feet tucked under her on one side and the book spread open wide in her lap. Scanning the table of contents until she found an unfamiliar title, she turned to the page cited and began reading where she had left off the last time.

She was pleased to note that the poems were traditional, formally structured verse, composed with the reassuring discipline of rhyme and meter. None of that ridiculous free verse nonsense. Also, they had an appealing musicality to them, although the images were often surreal and the subjects the poems explored were highly unusual, bordering on the weird at times. Unfortunately, in her exhausted state the overall effect was soporific, and before long Penelope felt herself drifting off into flights of imagination that were distinct departures from the narrative line of the poem she was reading at the moment.

And then, without warning, she was in Dreamland again. Not just sleeping. Oh no, this was a place she immediately recognized from her last visit. *That* place. She had just come down on foot from a mountain peak where something terrible had transpired. She was distraught, wandering aimlessly through the narrow streets of a sea-side village—she didn't know its name.

But *what* had happened on the mountaintop, and why could she not remember it if it was so awful? All she knew was that she had to find the Weird Tales Museum. That absurd place! For some reason, she needed to go back there and fetch something.

She sensed that it lay just ahead, one or two more streets further. All around her flowed a constant stream of people passing in either direction. They all looked poor, bedraggled, dirty, and grotesque, like pathetic smelly beggars in some god-awful miserable third-world country. Ahead she spotted a dilapidated wooden building rising up before a stone cliff. Ah, that was the place. A yellow silken banner draped across the upper portion of the structure proclaimed in huge letters "Lovecraft's Creatures in Fact and Fancy—A Retrospective Exhibition," and below that, in small letters, the couplet "How dull the wretch, whose philosophic mind / Disdains the pleasures of fantastic kind." Below this, she observed a public entrance with a ticket window and turnstiles. She reached into the pocket of her night-gown and was pleased to feel a quantity of coins and a few bills of currency. Pulling out a fistful, she slapped the money on the counter and asked the dimwitted-looking girl behind the glass if that was enough to cover one adult admission.

"More than enough, ma'am. It's only five cents."

Penelope slid a nickel across the counter to the girl, noting as she did so that it had a very old design and was nearly worn smooth. The girl handed her a ticket and smiled broadly, revealing a gaping hole where her front teeth ought to have been.

"Enjoy your visit," said the girl mechanically, as if she'd said it a thousand times before. She was already looking at the next customer in line, having immediately dismissed Penelope from her mind.

"Oh, I'll just be a minute," Penelope replied. "I'm not staying." As if the girl gave a damn what Penelope did.

Inside the vestibule it was dark and cool, the relatively confined area given an exaggerated sense of spaciousness by the echoes of ris-ing and falling voices from the crowd. She knew exactly where she was going and made a beeline for the women's restroom. The last time she had been here she had left something important in the la-dies' room, something she needed to pass on to Mandy Peaslee. As before, the restroom seemed more like a mildly flooded series of natural caves than a man-made room in a building. There were var-ious degrees of moisture on the floor, and it was even darker than it had been out in the vestibule, with irregular walls of rippling rock and strange little chambers branching off in all directions. She hoped she didn't get lost. It took her a while to find the thing she was seeking, and she began to despair at her odds of success; but then suddenly she spied it, sitting on a polished granite counter across from a row of toilet stalls—just where she'd left it.

The blood-soaked scrapbook.

Amazing, she reflected, that even with all the people coming and going, nobody had taken it. Especially considering all the seedy-looking characters in this town. That was indeed lucky.

She snatched it up, tucked it safely under one arm, and dashed from the restroom and toward the museum exit. But along the way, something caught her eye: a brightly lit series of display cases over by the snack bar. Some kind of special attraction designed to stop traffic as it flowed out the doors, keeping the guests hanging around the snack bar long enough that they would eventually get hungry and buy something.

Burnished brass letters mounted on the rocky wall above the display cases gave the title of this mini−exhibit as: "Night−Gaunts: Horrific Fact or Harmless Fiction?" The exhibit consisted of numer− ous portraits, art reproductions, and blocks of narrative text—all mounted on white panels—alongside a hodge−podge of vintage ar− tifacts that were allegedly associated with the legendary creatures. Penelope noted a black−and−white photograph of the actress Re− becca Pascal, looking serene and stately in a shimmering full−length silver gown. And she remembered from her last stay in this strange land that she had found a page or two of snapshots of these mon− strous demon−like creatures, these "night−gaunts," in Rebecca's stained scrapbook. The panel next to Pascal's image stated: "It was rumored among the Arkham cognoscenti that the acclaimed film star had engaged in secret commerce with the heinous black−winged entities and had even been visited by them on several occasions." The photographs Penelope had briefly examined lent a certain credibility to that claim.

Moving to the next display case, Penelope was stopped dead in her tracks by another vintage black−and−white photograph, this one of a small boy whom she immediately recognized as her little broth− er, James. He had tragically disappeared one afternoon when he was only five years old and she was but a teenager, and had never been seen again. Presumed dead. And then it came back to her: *he* was the long−lost "loved one" she had been reunited with the last time she was here. But it hadn't lasted long, the wonderful gift of his return. The night−gaunts had taken him by force once more on the moun− taintop. Despite her best efforts, she had been unable to prevent this new abduction by the hateful beasts. And now he was lost to her again, hidden away in some unknown, concealed part of this terrible land.

How eerie to see his sweet face there in the display case, sur−

rounded by old yellowed newspaper clippings about the mysterious disappearance. It didn't seem real; more like a nightmare that she would wake up from any second now.

She couldn't bear to read the story of his kidnapping and the ensuing search for his body; could not tolerate reliving all that negative emotion. Turning away, she walked briskly toward the exit, pretending she hadn't seen the display.

Outside, the day was warm and bright, with people milling about everywhere, some of them flowing toward the entrance turnstiles, others looking for further amusements, having already exhausted the attractions of the Weird Tales Museum, and a few of them with families of small children in tow, in search of food and drink.

Although it had no purpose being there, Penelope stumbled across her car parked on a side street near the museum, but it was not the mundane modern sedan she drove to work every day in her waking life. Instead, it was the ancient green Triumph convertible sports car she had owned in college. The trunk lid was open, and inside the trunk was a box of her papers from the library, stuff from the Pascal Archive she'd brought home to work on. At that instant, she knew exactly what to do, forcefully shoving the scrapbook into the already stuffed box of papers. That way, when she returned the papers to her office, she would have the scrapbook with her to give to Mandy so it could be cleaned and restored. Mandy would know just what to do with it; she had a gift for making things right. Penelope would think of it no more.

CHAPTER XIV

They followed Agnes down the rutted road, until they came to a bridge that crossed a silent river. Simon was the first to notice the chill breeze that wafted from the flow of water, and he cautiously espied the woodland that engulfed what remained of the roadway some distance from them. One portion of his wizard's brain sensed a subtle suggestion of sinister aura, and he prided himself that some vile essence of this alchemy was aimed maliciously at him. Always relishing the breaking of rules, Simon hoped that his being in dreamland, in any way, shape, or form, was an outlandish violation, a thing forbidden. Edith had obviously been mistaken that, because he was a warlock, Simon would find any kind of welcome in this dreamland of witchery. Perhaps it was his inhuman Sesquan nature that caused the infringement he sensed. He was unaware that he was chortling out loud until his companions turned to look at him suspi‐ciously.

The sound of tolling bells came to them on the scented breeze. Rebecca, peering into the woodland, caught sight of a white struc‐ture that was mostly concealed by the growth of trees; and her curi‐osity was piqued, for she could not imagine what kind of tabernacle could exist in this dreamland of witchery. Steadily, she crossed the bridge, not turning to see if the others had followed her. Simon was the last to set foot onto the bridge; and as he began to cross over the river, the chill that rose from the water encased his inhuman flesh. He could detect, in that cool air, a kind of alchemy; and when his large ears became aware of a murmuring in the flowing water, Simon could not help but stop and lean across the barrier. At first, he could not comprehend the oscillating shape that seemed to summon him playfully beneath the water; and then that shape took on a more solid form, and Simon knew that he was watching a kind of eidolon of that which is known as the Crawling Chaos. The figure of pitch and shadow lifted its right arm until its hand emerged slightly into the outer air; and something in the glistening beauty of that hand so enticed the beast of Sesqua Valley that Simon found himself bending to it, so as to touch his mouth to its palm.

Rebecca and Agnes turned, startled at the sound of a startled yelp that was followed by a loud splash. Agnes, running back onto the bridge, peered into the river and saw the two figures that wrapped their forms beneath the water. She screamed Simon's name as he was dragged away, wrapped in blackness, his struggling form rushing beneath the bridge and away from his companions. Crying in protest, Rebecca raised her hand and tried to call out a potent spell, but a wave of daemonic force pushed out of the water and took hold of her brain, so that she was overwhelmed with dizziness and fell to the ground. She gagged and cursed until warm arms wound around her frame, as Agnes, beside her, helped Rebecca to a standing position.

"It was an aspect of Nyarlathotep," Agnes whispered.

"Yes," Rebecca answered, panting. "He is the one creature who is able to crawl into this dream realm of witchery. Simon's presence here would provide a natural allure to the Strange Dark One. We have lost the beast and must continue without him. Come, let us investigate this edifice."

"Wait!" Agnes cried as she noticed something on the ground. She bent and picked up the lean red flute that had been Simon's favorite instrument. "It must have slipped out of his jacket's inner pocket," she whispered, more to herself than to Rebecca. A forlorn expression tainted her eyes as she brought the tip of the instrument to her mouth; but she found that she did not have the energy required to breath music through the implement, and so she sequestered it within the deep pocket of her dress.

The women moved away from the river and into woodland, away from the chilly river wind and into a place of calm and quietude. Stopping at one mammoth tree, Rebecca ran her hands over its patches of bright green moss, until her hands were stained; and then she rubbed those hands over her face, moaning at the sensations that sank into her flesh. Agnes did not move immediately as Rebecca lifted one hand to her, and she trembled slightly as the older woman stepped to her and pressed her tainted hands onto Agnes's countenance. She could feel the substance of the moss sink into the texture of her face and find her brain; and she marveled as her vision transformed and everything around her became sharper in focus. Leaning toward Agnes, Rebecca kissed the younger woman's eyes and clasped her hand.

They moved through the woods until they stood at the entrance of the building. A kind of hush enveloped the dreamland as the women eyed the diminutive cowled figures that watched them. The quietude enhanced a quality that was so unearthly that Agnes thought it must be some aura especial to this dreamworld. Without waiting for Rebecca to join her, Agnes moved past the small hooded creatures and entered the white edifice. She found herself inside a kind of foyer wherein candles burned on tall wrought-iron candelabras. Walking past these, Agnes pushed open the double doors of bright red wood and entered a vaulted chamber; but rather than finding the pews she expected, she saw that the chamber was filled with a long table of dark wood that was covered with books and manuscripts and scrolls. She walked into the silent place and stopped at a small table on which she found a chalice of white gold that contained a small amount of dark red liquid. Before Rebecca, who had followed her into the room, could stop her, Agnes raised the chalice to her mouth and drank.

CHAPTER XV

Mandy's modest little apartment, situated on the western slope of the historic French Hill district of Arkham, had a splendid view of the city considering the low rent she paid. When the weather was fine, Mandy made a habit of enjoying a leisurely glass of wine out on the balcony before dinner. She preferred red wine—Pinot Noir or Merlot—but now and then for the sake of variety she went with Chardonnay, and of course, always a cigarette or two to accompany it. This was her favorite part of the day. She felt like she had earned this half−hour of relaxation, gazing out at the city sprawled below, sipping the rich essence of the grape, watching bands of cloud stretched out along the horizon gradually turn from pink to red to purple as the sun dipped below the hills and night came on.

But this afternoon she just couldn't quiet her mind. That idiotic Dr. Lang had her in a total panic. Shooting off his mouth like that, telling people about the photos she'd sold him, and even identifying her as the source. What in the hell was he thinking? Had the man lost all reason? She felt very vulnerable having anyone other than Lang know about the night−gaunt images. What if the photos were traced back to the university and ultimately to her? She'd be in deep trouble. And then he had the gall to ask about negatives and other prints! If there were any—and she made a mental note to find that out as soon as she could—they would act as damning proof that the stolen photos had come from the Pascal Archive. The smartest thing she could do would be to locate them immediately and bury them in some deep hole far from Miskatonic University. But first she would have to come up with a good, believable reason why she should be allowed to rummage through the hundreds of photographs and negatives now being inventoried by Penelope. And what if Penelope came upon additional night-gaunt images before Mandy had a chance to remove the telltale items from the collection? That was another huge risk. What a mess! It was moments like this that made her glad she had a travel bag in the closet, stuffed with cash. Just in case a quick exit from Arkham became advisable.

Feeling too tired to deal with any real cooking, she heated a frozen pizza for dinner. Normally she would have added fresh veggies or a salad, but not tonight. She would deal with the Dr. Lang situation tomorrow. Right now, all she wanted was to numb her mind, to distract herself with something irrelevant and meaningless. Ah, she knew just the thing: that drippy book of poems by the old witch woman Edith Gnome. It had put her to sleep before and would do so again. Slipping into pajamas, Mandy found the book and sprawled out on the bed with it.

Atmospheric and vaguely disturbing, Gnome's poems were eerie, even spooky. As she read them, she had the uncanny feeling that the creepy grad student—what did Penelope say his name was? Charles Morelle, that was it—was present there, in the room with her, spying on her. Feeling foolish as she did so, Mandy searched the apartment, checking closets, looking under the bed, peeking behind the shower curtain, assuring herself that he was not there. Yet when she returned to the book, the feeling of being watched persisted—as if he were looking over her shoulder as she read. Vexed, she flung the book aside, rolled over on her back, stretched out on top of the covers, and closed her eyes. A moment later, she was asleep and dreaming. In a vision she saw herself as a free-spirited young girl in a long, flowing white dress of simple cotton, seated on the back of a gargantuan moth whose body was covered in brilliant hues of glow-in-the-dark fur, coursing through the skies over a dark and desolate plain someplace very far from Arkham.

She had been there before. She knew where she was. In the Dreamlands, on a mission of mercy, journeying toward Penelope

Armitage, who had also transitioned to this strange realm on this very same night. Together, the two of them would liberate Penelope's little brother, James, from the evil herd of night−gaunts that had cruelly spirited him away. She must not fail. Penelope was counting on her, even if she didn't realize it. In the depths of her soul, Penelope had called out for Mandy to rectify this terrible situation, and rectify it she would. Mandy was filled with the purest joy imaginable as she embarked on this highly noble errand. Nothing could equal the exaltation she experienced soaring through the air, racing to her good friend's aid.

Chapter XVI

Agnes fell into a void of utter darkness, in which all her senses were numb and useless. Her entire body was tormented by tingling sensations, and she felt like some kind of shapeless amoeba, given how her form seemed to contort and spread. Blurred globes of various hues drifted over her, and one began to call her name; and as Agnes intensified her focus, the pale globe took on the form of Edith Gnome's face and its moving mouth. The globe then became a blur, as high-pitched humming accompanied the distant playing of a flute. As the pale orb became solid once more, Agnes saw that it was the sinister visage of Rebecca Pascal that watched her. Beside the witch, one of the hooded dwarves held Simon's red flute to its shapeless mouth.

The music stopped as Agnes sat up. Rebecca, smoothing a hand through the younger woman's hair, said, "You should know better than to drink anything found in the dreamland of witchery. Haven't you heard the legends or read the old fairy tales? Poison is a favorite witch-tool with which to corrupt and incapacitate. A poisoned apple or needle will escort one into a state of semi-death. An elixir in a decorative cup will usher one into a state of deadly sleep from which there is no awakening. Had we not known the formula with which to revive you, your mortal heart would have ceased its tremor. Be wary in this realm of dream, young woman."

Agnes reached for Simon's flute and removed it from the hooded figure's hand, and then she looked upward as, from some unseen region, bells began to toll. The small cowled creatures moved away and shuffled to a spiral staircase, which they began to climb. With curiosity piqued, Agnes rose and offered her hand to Rebecca. The gesture seemed to surprise the older woman, who nonetheless reached out to clasp the proffered hand; and together the women climbed the winding stairway that took them into a spacious area of smothered illumination, where shadows crawled like remembered things across white walls. Dim radiance tried to peek beyond thick clouds of incense smoke, and one feeble ray finally freed itself so as to fall upon the oblong box that rested in one corner. The women watched quietly as a formless thing wrapped in a robe as red as sunset flame lifted itself out of the casket and fell onto the floor; and Agnes turned at the sound of low humming that came from some other section of the chamber, where she espied the hooded huddled crea-tures who moved subtly to and fro as they breathed fitfully a kind of wordless hymn.

The shapeless white form squirmed a little across the floor, tan-gled within its scarlet gown, reminding Agnes of a monstrous worm that has issued from some nameless pit of death. She watched, and saw that portions of the pallid flesh began to darken and change in texture as the creature folded its form and then, shuddering, began to lift itself erect. It rose, it rose—and the women took in the antique clothes that were mostly hidden within the folds of the crimson cloak, the hood of which concealed the figure's head. From out that hood a pair of animated eyes observed them, and Agnes thought she had never seen eyes that contained such melancholy. The figure, now obviously discerned as male, lifted a pair of small hands to the hood and pushed it off its dome, revealing a mass of dark wavy hair atop a wide forehead. A small moustache grew over thin lips, and the throat was adorned with a green silk cravat. The gentleman raised his arms, which were hidden within the wide sleeves of his crimson robe, to the women, and he genuflected to them.

"My dear ladies, I thank you for disturbing my long rest. I had a dream of the pealing of sonorous bells; but they have stopped their clanging now, and all is silence. This is a lonely place, and I have slept as if in my tomb, not moving; and any creature looking on me would fancy me dead." He smiled coyly as he stepped nearer to Agnes and offered her his hand. "I am Edgar." The young woman allowed the fellow to take her hand, which he kissed tenderly.

"I am Miss Aspinwall, and my companion is Miss Pascal. How long have you lingered here, within this dreamland of witchery?"

He released her hand and shrugged. "I have lost all comprehension of time; nor do I believe that Time, as once I understood it, can exist within this dream realm. I have a faint memory of falling into a void of shadow as I was conjuring an alchemy of poetry, with which I often evoked supernatural matter. But perhaps that memory is nothing more than elusive reverie, and I have dropped into a dream within a dream. Ah, it feels good to stretch! But I have breathed enough of cloistered air and long to extend my arms and legs beyond these unhallowed walls. Lead me, sweet ladies, to the outside realm."

Rebecca studied the fellow for some silent moments with a curious smile playing on her mouth; and then she bowed to him and said, "Follow me, good sir. Use caution—we wouldn't want you to trip by stepping on your scarlet gown."

"Stop," Edgar commanded. "I think that I was wrapped inside this gown as a kind of jest, for certainly it does not suit me. See, I unfasten it and slide it from my form. It needs to encase a lovelier figure than mine own. I think . . ." He approached Rebecca and touched a hand to the fabric of her dress; and then he turned to regard the hooded dwarves and gently clapped his hands. "Assist me, imps." The small creatures oozed as one toward them, watching as the fellow began to work at Rebecca's clothing. Small dark hands moved over the woman's gown and tugged, and then the creatures backed away as the dress fell from the woman's body. Edgar's dark eyes shimmered, and his head bent to the woman's neck, which his nostrils sniffed. Lowering his head, he kissed the nape of Rebecca's neck; and then he raised his scarlet gown and dropped it over the older woman's structure of flesh and bone. Edgar backed away and admired his work. "You are a poem," he sighed, "a sonnet."

Leaning to him, Rebecca pressed her lips against his eyes; and then she moved from them and began to descend the spiral staircase.

CHAPTER XVII

Drifting aimlessly away from the Weird Tales Museum with no concept of where she was headed, Penelope walked along the crowded streets of the seaport town in what she sensed was a northerly direction, swept along by the masses of people as much as by any conscious volition of her own. She was numbed by what she'd just seen in the museum display case—the few known dreadful facts surrounding her little brother's disappearance so many years ago—and all she could think about was that, regardless of how steep were the odds of success, she must at least try to locate and rescue him. She had found him once before in this strange realm, in a mysterious wood where he'd magically emerged from a fog bank, and they had spent a fine day together, but then something had compelled her to seek out a mountain pass whence she was led to believe it might be possible for her to escort James back to the waking world, the real world of everyday life.

And that's where the terrible event had transpired. A swarm of night–gaunts had descended from the sky at sunset and attacked them. Try as she might to fight them off with a small sword she had bartered from a devilishly handsome pirate in a seedy waterfront tavern, she was overmatched and could not prevent the ugly daemonic creatures from snatching little Jimmy in their fierce claws and carrying him away to an unknown fate. There must be some way to determine where he was being held and secure his escape from his captors. Surely someone here in Dreamland could help her, tell her how it could be managed, send her in the right direction, maybe even accompany her on this mission. She must find that person at all costs.

The smell of cooking and a weathered sign hanging on an old wooden frame building proclaiming "Public Fish House" caught her attention. She was much in need of refreshment, being tired, hungry, and thirsty all at the same time. The thought of sitting down to a hot meal and a cold drink was very appealing. The place didn't look like much—nothing in this crummy town did—it was shabby, run-down, needing paint and repairs, but the sundry aromas wafting out the establishment's open doors were all pleasant and seafood was pretty hard to get wrong. If it was freshly caught and adequately cooked, it would be edible and possibly delicious. Determined to take her chances on the fare being of sufficient quality, Penelope entered the eatery and got in line behind a dozen others who were waiting to place their orders at the counter. Reading from the numerous menus plastered about on the walls, Penelope decided on batter-fried halibut with a side bowl of clam chowder and a glass of beer. She would have preferred ice water, but the menus all clearly stated that water was not an option. How odd, she thought. Perhaps sanitation was a problem in the town.

Like admission to the museum, the price of a meal seemed ridiculously low. She slid a beat-up silver quarter across the Formica counter, and a burly man in a grease-stained apron handed her a nickel in change along with a receipt that he had handwritten on a grubby slip of paper with a dull pencil stub.

"That'll be right up for ye in about five minutes, lovely miss."

Being called "lovely miss" took her totally by surprise, making her feel young and feminine again, if but for a second. That was a rare thing for Penelope these days, feeling like a woman. Most days she felt like a withered, genderless shell of her former self. A lot of water had passed under the bridge since her college days.

"Thank you, sir," she replied, taking her ticket and stepping aside to wait for her number to be called. Once her order was up, she carried the tray over to an empty table by the window that looked out on the ocean. It was a delightful view, with large waves crashing gustily on the shore, ships out on the water bobbing like corks, screeching gulls wheeling through the air, and countless children of all ages, running, screaming, and laughing across the sandy beach. She took her time, enjoying the meal, after which she returned to her pointless task of wandering the streets, still headed north as the sun began to set, realizing at some point that she would need accommodations for the night. A large white inn, unexpectedly decent in appearance, presented itself to view. She saw no point in looking further, doubting she would find a better place to stay than this one.

"How much would a room be for the night?" she inquired of the gnarled old woman who tended the front desk.

The hag looked her up and down suspiciously, then asked, "Is it just you, then, madame?"

"Yes, only me. I am quite alone in this world." As if she had some uncouth fellow stashed outside that she would sneak into her room once she'd gotten the key, like a common whore—the absurdity of the idea!

"It's twenty-five cents then, in advance."

"I'll take it." Penelope pulled another silver quarter from her pocket and handed it to the woman, who stared closely at it, bit the coin on one edge to test the authenticity of the metal, and then took an iron key of antique design from a peg on a board and led Penelope upstairs to her room on the second floor.

"Absolutely no male visitors allowed at any time, and no singing or playing of musical instruments after ten."

"Not to worry, I'll be as quiet as a churchmouse."

The old woman laughed heartily at that—too heartily, Penelope thought.

"A bleeding churchmouse!" she roared, slapping her fat thighs with the meaty palms of her hands. And with that unnecessary indignity, the woman left her.

Penelope washed her face and hands in a small porcelain sink in one corner of the room and dried them off on a fluffy white towel she found in the cabinet under the sink. Further exploring the room, she discovered some articles of women's clothing hanging in the room's only closet, apparently abandoned by the previous occupant. Among the garments were several fancy cotton print dresses trimmed in lace—all of them long, old-fashioned affairs that came down to her ankles, as well as some similarly vintage-style blouses, vests, sweaters, and jackets. Although normally she wouldn't dream of wearing a stranger's clothing, she felt an odd compulsion to change into one of these charming old dresses. Selecting a dark design highlighted with a delicate pattern of lighter-hued flowers, she slipped out of her nightgown and into the new dress. Only after she had done this did she realize she had failed to pull the window shades down and had thereby treated the men on the beach to an unscheduled peep show. Oh, well—too late for precaution; let them ogle her in her underwear. There were worse misfortunes in this world for a woman to endure.

Night came on quickly, and with the spread of darkness across the land and the warm glow of a full moon out over the glittering water, she began to feel uncharacteristically restless. Taking a sweater from the closet and grabbing her room key, Penelope set out impulsively, with no destination in mind other than a change of scenery. She walked briskly onto the beach and turned north, thinking she would follow the coastline until something interesting happened. Hearing the roar of the waves as they broke to her left, and breathing deeply of the salt-scented air that swirled all about her, she weaved her way around rugged outcroppings of black stone and carefully picked a path through broad areas of sand strewn with driftwood and the shards of broken logs that had washed up on the shore from countless shipwrecks over the years.

Soon she was far from the town, on a smooth, flat, isolated beach that stretched ahead for miles without another human being in sight, the land to her right now totally obscured in inky darkness, with only glints of moonlight on the waves to her left and the sheen of wet sand below her feet to show the way forward. That's when she first detected a small patch of red radiance on the beach a long distance ahead. As she continued to approach the mysterious light, it slowly took on form, and when she was within earshot, she saw that the glowing object was in fact a large bonfire, around which numerous black–cloaked feminine figures were gathered in a large circle. Each cowled woman held in her right hand a burning candle, her sinister hand shielding the flame from the stiffly gusting wind. These women, she instinctively knew, were witches in the act of practicing their craft. The hour was precisely midnight, and she'd innocently strayed into their secret ceremony. All the women turned in unison toward Penelope, all eyes now stared at her in silence as she reached the outer edge of their communal circle. One of the women, clearly the leader from her air of authority, stepped out of the circle and swept across the sand toward Penelope, saying in a voice both warm and fearsome, "Welcome, my dear. We have long awaited your arrival."

Remarkably, Penelope felt as if she belonged there among these women, as if she were somehow one of them. And then, for the first time since she had entered the hotel room earlier that evening, she suddenly came to her senses. Had she been under some sort of spell—in a trance state—these past few hours? What on earth had possessed her, of all people, to do something so out of character as to wander the streets of a strange city alone, after dark, like a mindless teenager in search of fun? And worse, to set off impulsively on a foolish jaunt along a dark beach in an area overrun by thieves, beggars, molesters, cut–throat pirates, and worse? Was she mad? *Good Lord!*

"*You've* been expecting *me?* That's absurd. You don't even know me!"

The enchantress smiled patiently, and Penelope had to admit to herself that the woman seemed both sincere and well–intentioned. "Ah, you're mistaken, Penelope Armitage. We know you very well—better than you know yourself—and we love you like a sister."

"Heavens! One absurdity after another. Okay, if you know me so well, why am I here, in this ridiculous land, on this stupid beach? Answer me that one, missy."

"You are in search of a dear one who was taken from you—not once, but twice in your life. The first time was many years ago when you were quite young, just entering adulthood. The second time was but a few weeks ago when you were briefly reunited with that loved one in this very place, which we inhabitants call Dreamland. Your heart is breaking for the loss of your little brother, James, and you've come here in the desperate hope that you will be able to find him and liberate him from an evil force that conceals him from you and others of the waking world. You hope to bring him back with you to live out his life in that other realm. Am I correct?"

This got Penelope's attention. So the woman did know something about her after all—but how? Had someone tipped her off? "Okay, I'll grant you that much. I am looking for Jimmy. But still, you don't know me. Not really."

"Oh, I do know you. I have known you all your life. As have these women who now burn the candle for your benefit. We have watched over you every day and night since you were an infant in the cradle. There is one member of our company who is not present yet—a most exalted being. I have summoned her so that she may aid you in your search and she is in transit now, wending her way from a remote region, one that is, in fact, another dreamland little known to men and women of the waking world: a dreamland of witchery. She journeys this very moment through a transitional dimension that lies between this dreamland of common men and women and the dreamland of witchery, a dark domain not easily crossed. But she has special transport: the giant moth–like creature that is called 'The Herald of the Morning.' On this creature's back the exalted one soars through the skies of the transitional realm. She will arrive shortly."

"Good grief! You actually expect me to believe such poppy-cock?"

"Believe it or do not. You'll see with your own eyes."

"I'll believe it when I see it."

"That you will, my dear."

While they had conversed, the cowled women chanted in a gut-tural language that Penelope did not recognize. The leader of the witches now turned her back on Penelope and strode to the roaring bonfire at the circle's center. Facing the blaze, the enchantress—

whom Penelope considered delusional if not actually insane—raised up her arms and addressed the moon above.

"Goddess on high! We seek your loving power and protection. Descend now and join us, lending your sublime spirit to our combined humble spirits, that collectively we may bring to our beloved sister Penelope a resolution to sorrow. We beseech thee, oh Goddess!"

Sure, thought Penelope, *the goofy moon is going to come down and help me find Jimmy. In a pig's eye!* But her cynical smirk instantly transformed into open-mouthed awe when a column of brilliant white luminescence shot down from the glowing lunar orb and hit the surface of a broad, flat rock situated at the edge of the fire—a rock that Penelope now realized served as an altar. The enchantress grabbed a burnt stick from out of the ashy periphery of the fire and used its sooty charcoal tip to inscribe an occult symbol on the face of the stone. Then the cowled women began to walk past the marked stone, one by one, each woman pouring a small amount of hot wax from her candle onto the black traced symbol. By the time the last woman had done so, a sizable puddle of semi-molten wax had built up on the stone. The leader of the witches then scooped up a handful of this still warm wax and began to knead it gently in her hands, squeezing and pinching the malleable lump until it took on the shape of a small boy, modeled in miniature. The woman held up the figurine for Penelope to see: it was the spitting image of James, rendered in wax.

Penelope gasped involuntarily. Maybe the woman had been telling the truth all along. Maybe she did know all about Jimmy, not to mention Penelope herself.

Then the enchantress lifted the wax figure high above her head, as if presenting it proudly to the moon.

"This, Goddess, is the child we seek! Bring your exalted daughter to our aid so that we may secure the boy! We thank you in advance for your abundant kindness, oh Goddess!" And with that, the witch dashed the wax figure into the fire, where it bubbled and sizzled, releasing oily billows of gray smoke that drifted away in the ocean breeze.

Tears streamed down Penelope's face. Too stunned to speak, she turned away from the circle of women and began to walk slowly back down the beach toward the lights of the town and her hotel.

A voice she recognized as that of the enchantress called out after her.

"Penelope: you'll find the exalted one in the room where it is always sunset. Join her there at noon tomorrow, and have faith. She will help you. I promise that much."

Chapter XVIII

It was the wee hours of the morning by the time Penelope returned to the hotel. She stepped out of the ankle−length, old−fashioned dress and tossed it into a wicker laundry basket. Walking along the surf had left the hem damp and coated with sand. She washed her beach−stained feet in the bathtub and put on her nightgown, its dry flannel a luxury against her skin after the soggy dress. Then, utterly exhausted, she lay down on top of the bed covers and fell asleep. A dream came in which she watched Mandy rinse the pages of the bloody scrapbook clean in a large stone basin full of water. Mandy told Penelope this was the "Fount of Tears," and explained that soaking the pages in the basin would remove all sorrows that had seeped into the scrapbook. Penelope mused, *That's what Mandy does; she removes the sorrow;* but she did not share this thought with Mandy.

The next morning Penelope put on another dress from the clos−et—this one a plain cotton shift that came to her knees—and went down to the lobby for breakfast. She was enjoying a repast of buttered muffin and black tea when an elaborately costumed gypsy woman strayed into the dining room and headed straight for her table.

"Oh dear . . ." muttered Penelope, softly enough not to be overheard.

"Good morning to you, madame," said the gypsy. "I have something here that will be of great interest to you."

"I sincerely doubt that, my dear, but go ahead, try me."

"If I may," inquired the gypsy, gesturing to an empty chair.

"Certainly. Be my guest."

"Is that one bothering you any, miss?" called out the gnarled hag tending the front desk.

"Not really. At least, not yet she isn't. It's okay."

"Fine then, have it your way. Do tell me if she gets to be an annoyance, and I'll give 'er the bum's rush."

"I'll do that—thank you. Now, you were saying?" continued Penelope, turning her attention back to the gypsy woman now seated across from her.

The gypsy produced a deck of cards from the folds of her silken garment. She began placing them face up in a row across the tablecloth, noisily flicking each card as she laid it down for maximum dramatic effect. Penelope studied the images on the cards. They were unfamiliar to her. Definitely not standard playing cards. Perhaps some kind of Tarot cards.

"Are you going to tell my fortune?" asked Penelope. "And if so, what will it cost me?"

"No, not your fortune. That is a foolish parlor trick done by frauds and fakes. I am going to impart an important message from a friend. This costs you nothing. It is a gift."

"Okay. I'll hold you to your word. No surprises at the end, eh?"

"No surprises, I assure you."

Penelope stared at the cards a while longer. "What now?" she asked.

"Pick up a card and look at it. Then tell me what it represents."

Penelope picked up the card on the far left. It had a picture of a grinning skeleton holding a scythe. "A cheery one, this. I'd say that represents Death."

"And now tell me the first terrible thing that comes to your mind."

"Okay. That's easy. My father dying a week after he retired. Poor man never got to enjoy his retirement after a lifetime of hard work."

"Good answer. Pick up another card and do the same."

The next card Penelope picked up had a picture on it of a

ghoulish, semi–human creature surrounded by leaping flames. The thing had long fangs, wild eyes, and a pointed tail. It reminded her of the lost souls that Dante wrote about in the *Inferno*. "I'd say this is a devil of some sort, a demon from hell, if you believe in such things, and it makes me think of that poor family that was killed in a car crash last week: a mother, the father, their three small kids—all their lives snuffed out by a senseless drunk driver."

"Excellent. Please go on."

"Okay, although I hardly see the point." Penelope worked her way through the cards, naming the things depicted on them and de–scribing to the gypsy the abominable thoughts that came to mind when she looked at them. Laying the last card down, she looked into the gypsy's dark eyes and waited for an explanation.

"The images on the cards are all negative forces, as you no doubt observed. And the terrible events you revealed are likewise negative forces. The pairing of these complementary negative forces creates a positive force. Two negatives cancel each other out and result in a positive. Through this magick ritual you become blessed and pro–tected. The blessing will be with you in the days that follow, watch–ing over you as you embark on a most perilous endeavor."

"Really? That's it? Honestly, it seems a bit weak to me."

"There is one who is coming to aid you in this dangerous enter–prise. She may be easily viewed in a negative light in the waking world where you best know her, due to the many irregularities in her dealings with others and certain ethical considerations; but that is a shallow, superficial view of her being, and of no great importance. In *this* realm, the dreamland, this same one is an enlightened being, a person of high stature. The negative forces of her mundane life in the waking world cancel out the negative forces that bedevil you here, and together these two negatives result in a positive energy. It is the same with her and the negative forces that afflict you, as with the cards and your terrible thoughts. The two negative forces cancel each other out and in the end there will be only goodness."

"Good Lord! I'm sorry, but that's got to be the lamest thing I've ever heard."

"Say what you will, my dear, but it's the truth."

Her brow wrinkled with cynicism, Penelope sipped at her tea and rolled her eyes while the gypsy woman gently swept up the cards, returned them to the hidden place in the depths of her exotic garment, and gracefully exited the room, smiling back at Penelope all the while.

Chapter XIX

Mandy passed from the transitional realm into the dreamland during the first few moments of sunrise and traversed the western skies for several hours before arriving at the port town of Dylath−Leen. Under the light of dreamland's sun, her mount, the gargantuan moth known as "The Herald of the Morning," was no longer a veritable rainbow of vividly glowing hues but rather a nondescript gray. As such, the creature was far less ostentatious a sight and commanded little attention from the local inhabitants as Mandy directed it toward her destination: the building housing the Weird Tales Museum. Hardly anyone noticed when moth and girl landed on the museum's rooftop, and those who did observe this minor event in the town's history paid it little mind. Climbing down off the moth's back, Mandy approached the lepidopteran's head and tenderly placed her hands on its proboscis, stroking it as she spoke.

"Hush now and do not fret. I will recall you when the need arises, but for now you are free to rest. Sleep deeply, dear one, for you have served me well. In due time we will soar again through dark and remote skies. Until then, I bid you goodbye." She bent forward and kissed the furry spot between its huge compound eyes, then backed away. When she was twenty paces distant, the completely still creature suddenly collapsed into a mound of ash which the wind off the sea quickly dispersed, leaving behind no trace. Mandy smiled, knowing she would see the moth again someday and that it was only taking a temporary respite from life.

The streets below were crowded with all manner of pedestrians, as well as men and women pulling carts or driving horse-drawn wagons, none of whom bothered to look up at the young girl in the white gown as she slipped through an unlocked door on a rooftop utility hut and disappeared into the building.

At that moment, Penelope was making her way down Dylath-Leen's main street, although she didn't know that was the name of the town in which she found herself. After her absurd discussion with the gypsy woman at breakfast, Penelope had set out to explore the town, hoping to solve the riddle the enchantress on the beach had posed to her in the little remaining time. The leader of the witch coven had told Penelope that she would meet at noon today with a person who would help her find Jimmy; that was less than an hour from now. The enchantress had assured her that this important meeting would take place "in the room where it is always sunset." What the hell did that mean? The only place she could think of where it might always be sunset would be on a planet that rotated in sync with its orbit around its sun, causing one side to be always in the dark while the other side was always lit. Along the boundary between the light and dark sides of such a planet, there would always be a condition similar to the moments before sunset on Earth. Well, she didn't know if there were any such planet anywhere in the universe, and even if there was, how could she possibly get there by noon?

Maybe she was being too literal. Perhaps the enchantress meant "where it is always sunset" symbolically. Penelope searched her memory; had she ever been any place in this bizarre land where it always *seemed as if* it were sunset, for whatever reason, even if it really wasn't?

"Aha!" she exclaimed loudly, causing several passersby on the street around her to turn and stare.

She *had* seen such a place, not far from where she was at that exact moment. It was down the street at the Weird Tales Museum. A small room-like scene was set up in one of the large display cases in the vestibule near the restrooms. The display was a life-sized replica of the editorial offices of *Weird Tales* magazine during the 1920s. The foreshortened "room"—which was about a dozen feet wide and no more than six feet deep—was fitted with office furnishings dating from the early twentieth century, including an old oak desk, wooden filing cabinets, a vintage letterpress machine, a cork bulletin board, and other historically appropriate items. An interior wall had been constructed immediately behind the desk with a paned window set in it. A couple feet behind that wall stood a second interior wall bearing a painted mural of a skyline that made viewers feel as if they were looking out the window at the city where the office was supposedly located: Chicago. The mural was lit by an off-stage rose-colored lamp that made the painted "sky" take on vivid shades of red and pink, creating the illusion that the sun had just set behind the black-silhouetted skyscrapers. And because the scene never changed, regardless of the actual time of day, it could be said that it was always the hour of sunset in that room. She had cracked the riddle!

Once she got there, Penelope was alarmed to find a line of people waiting to enter the museum. When it was finally her turn at the window, she paid her admission, grabbed the ticket from the clerk, and raced into the cool depths of the dimly lit lobby; there a large wall clock similar to those that had hung in her elementary school decades ago indicated that she had a mere fifteen minutes remaining until the appointed time. She decided that was just enough time for her to visit the ladies' restroom and still be punctual for the meeting.

Two minutes later Penelope emerged from the dank, cavernous restroom and was walking at a brisk pace up a long, sloping, tunnel-like corridor toward the vestibule when she noticed a small, unoccupied chamber situated off to her left. Curious as to what this side area might hold, she took an unplanned detour and peeked into the space. The odd little chamber was in the form of a semicircular cavity that seemingly had been carved from the solid white marble of the giant stone monolith against which the museum's main building had been constructed. Her attention was drawn to the back of the chamber where an elaborate tableau had been sculpted into the wall, with an ornate altar—like affair at its center that featured a fireplace. The indirect lighting in the chamber was soft and subdued, streaming vaguely from recessed fixtures high above. A small fire flickered weakly on the grate, near which were positioned a pair of comforta—ble—looking easy chairs. Something about this chamber was very soothing to Penelope. As rushed as she was, she stole a moment to sit in the chair nearest to the fire and enjoy the luxury of simply relaxing: slowly breathing in and out, and calming her mind. The chamber in—spired in Penelope a deep feeling of sanctuary, as if she could stay there indefinitely in peace and quiet, completely happy, free of all trouble.

Very tempting, she thought. *I could do just that; stay here for—ever, forgetting the world, forgetting life. Exist here outside of time in silence and harmony. Very tempting, indeed.*

But then she remembered the plight of her little brother. Duty called, and reluctantly she must answer. Rising from the chair, she forced herself to leave this sanctuary behind and return to the shad—owy corridor that would bring her back to the lobby; from there, it was but a few steps to the display case where very soon she would meet the mysterious being who might bring about her much desired reunion with Jimmy.

★

There was no one there when Penelope arrived at the display case housing the recreated editorial offices of *Weird Tales* magazine. That was a bit of a disappointment. After all the folderol with the enchantress and the gypsy woman, she had expected at least to be greeted, possibly even congratulated for solving the riddle and find—ing the place. *She* was on time; where was the mysterious person who would help her?

Pressing her nose against the glass window and shielding out the ceiling lights with her hands cupped over her eyes, she saw only an empty little room with a desk in the middle of it, on which sat an old manual typewriter and a green—shaded lamp. To one side of the desk stood a filing cabinet with papers stacked on top. She looked both ways up and down the length of the lobby, but nobody was approaching her. Rather, people were coming in and out of the corridor to the restrooms, or milling around the snack bar, or flowing in and out of the main part of the museum.

She was just about to turn away in dismay when a small motion inside the display area caught her attention. It was something lurking between the desk and the wall: some dark, round-shaped object, a portion of which extended an inch above the desk top. *What on earth could that be?* And then the roundish shape slowly rose into full view, and Penelope saw that it was a human head—that of a young girl with long, dark brown hair, a pretty face, and large, expressive eyes that were staring directly at her.

"Oh my God!" Penelope gasped. Immediately she recognized the face as being that of her coworker, Mandy, but a very young Mandy.

Mandy rotated her right hand in a circular motion in midair, pantomiming someone turning a door knob, then pointed to an unmarked door located a few feet from the edge of the display case.

Penelope nodded to show that she understood and walked over to the door, which she assumed provided access to the display. As such, it would be for the use of museum staff only and off-limits to the public. To her surprise, it was not locked. There were no guards around and none of the guests were watching her, so she gathered her courage, opened the door, and darted in. She found herself in a dusty storage area crammed full of strange old junk, so much of it that she could hardly make her way through the tightly packed clutter to the room where Mandy waited. There were ancient carriages with broken-spoked wheels, darkly tarnished medieval suits of armor, rolled Persian carpets, cardboard boxes stuffed with dilapidated antiquarian books, vintage electronic devices with frayed wires, oddly elongated glass vessels that looked as if they would have some obscure scientific use, and innumerable other time-worn objects whose purposes she could not even guess.

"Over here," called out Mandy as Penelope squeezed through narrow gaps between the jumbles of junk surrounding her. "You're almost there . . . just a bit further."

"I can hear you, my dear, but I can't see you. Oh my!" With very little provocation, a teetering wall of stuff lost its balance and came crashing down in front of Penelope—luckily away from and not toward her. "I could have been killed by that! Somebody needs to clean this place up—it's a hazard!"

Stepping over the dislodged artifacts littering her path, Penelope emerged into the relatively open space of the display area and found the girlish-looking Mandy, who had seated herself at the desk and was rummaging through a stack of papers she had taken down from the filing cabinet. Quickly sorting through a bundle of envelopes, Mandy pulled one out and removed several folded sheets of paper from it.

"Fancy meeting you here, Miss Peaslee. You're the last person I expected to encounter in this infernal habitat of drunken sailors and ne'er-do-wells."

Mandy looked up at Penelope with eyes that were bright and beaming with a generous sincerity. It was an expression that Penelope had not observed before in Mandy, who always seemed a bit weary and cynical in the waking world. But this was a much younger Mandy. She couldn't have been older than twelve or thirteen. Perhaps the vicissitudes of adult life had not yet worn her down.

"Aha!" exclaimed Mandy, returning to the papers in hand. "I was informed we would find this here: a letter from one of *Weird Tales'* most popular authors, Mr. Howard Phillips Lovecraft of Providence, Rhode Island, addressed to the magazine's editor, Mr. Farnsworth Wright. Supposed to hold special significance for you."

Mandy began reading in a soft, rapid, barely audible mumble, stopping mid-page to summarize the letter's content so far. "He's badgering Wright to send him a check for a story the magazine published months ago." This was followed by more mumbling by Mandy, and then another summary. "He goes on for quite a while, philosophizing about the proper place of human emotions in weird fiction narratives. He's keenly against anthropomorphizing the vast, cosmic, unknown Outside."

"Pray tell," said Penelope with more than a hint of sarcasm, "what has that to do with me? And why on earth should this Love—craft character even be writing to the editor of a trashy magazine about *me,* of all people? The man had no knowledge of me. For heaven's sake, I was born a full decade after his death!"

"Oh, he knew of you. At least here in dreamland, he did."

"Absurd. Please continue."

Mandy turned the page over and scanned the back side. "There's a long paragraph describing a visit to Copp's Hill Burying Ground in Boston. Okay, here we go. This part's about you; listen up. Love—craft writes: 'Please do me the favour of conveying to Miss Armitage my sincere apology for the many inconveniences and hardships that have been visited upon her family by these blasted creatures from the outer darkness. Assure her that, had it been within my power, I would have had them recalled immediately once they'd fulfilled their highly questionable mission and promptly banished to the hellish re—gion of their vile origin. However, I have no practical voice in such matters; I'm merely an idle dreamer and hold no sway with reigning occult powers and principalities. Do impress upon her my studied opinion that her best chances of finding the lad are in visiting that other dreamland which is the domain of witches and warlocks. This little—known land, I hear on good authority, is most likely where the fiendish night—gaunts and their ilk dare to maintain a stronghold for the detention of captive human children. I wish her every success in what is sure to prove a most challenging venture.' That's all he has to say on the subject."

"Another dreamland, besides this silly place? Nonsense! That's a fat lot of help," snorted Penelope.

"Oh, it's quite helpful," said Mandy, laying down the letter, "and simplifies things considerably. We're off to the dreamland of witchery!"

Chapter XX

As Agnes climbed down the winding staircase, she sensed a new element in the atmosphere but could not ascertain its origin. The air she breathed in seemed a bit heavier, and she fancied that shadows in corners were a bit darker than they had been when previously viewed. Gripping the railing, she turned for one brief moment to glance at Edgar, who was directly behind her; and she nodded in response to his tipping of his head to her as he smiled broadly.

"Watch your step, miss. This spiral has been known to be treacherous. We wouldn't want you to slip and bruise your pretty little head."

"I shall, sir, thank you. And I pass such caution on to you, for we wouldn't desire you to fall and bump your wide and noble brow." He frowned in confusion at her reply, and this made Agnes smile. She glided smoothly down to the ground level, where she was watched by the clutch of small, hooded figures. Rebecca had already vacated the edifice, and so Agnes passed through the doorways and joined the elder woman, who was bathing her face in the light of a moon that was now a curious blend of green and orange in color.

"Ah," whispered Edgar as he joined them, "the mystic moon, spilling her opiate beams onto our shadowed eyes. Look there—the playful bats, or things that resemble bats, darting between the shafts of narcotic light. Let us combine our talents and conjure a sorcerous tempest that will weave this unnatural lunar illumination into fantastic daemons to our view." Raising his hands, the fellow began to twitch his fingers as if suffering from a kind of epilepsy. Rebecca watched him in silence, frowning.

"Your wizardry is a little erratic, I fear. We need to combine the ghastly moonlight with the shadows of midnight, and then we can evoke something wicked."

"Must we wait for the chimes of midnight?" Edgar protested.

The elder woman gave him a knowing look. "It is always midnight in the dreamland of witchery, if one knows how to conjure it." As if to confirm her words, bells from the church steeple behind them began to announce the midnight hour. Edgar watched Rebecca, expecting her to move her hands in alchemical motion; and he was impressed to see that she worked her magick with her eyes alone, peering at the moonlight as vibrations of darkness spilled from the woman's orbs and wove into the lunar light. Coils of combined radiance and gloom coalesced and formed a monstrous visage that opened hateful silver eyes. Agnes cried out as she witnessed this enormous eidolon that aped the sardonic countenance of Simon Gregory Williams.

"What is this thing of evil?" Edgar exclaimed, inspiring Agnes to hold up her hand to silence him. She then motioned with that hand to the spectral visage that haunted the space above them, and made unto that image the Elder Sign. Simon's mouth parted as a flow of lava, red and orange and black, spilled from that cavity and engulfed the image, a flow that began to shape itself into what looked to be a twin-peaked mountain composed of dull black slate.

"There it is," Rebecca told them, nodding sagely, "our destination—the mountain K'nath. It is there, Agnes Aspinwall, that your mission will find its completion. We will find what we seek within a topmost cavern. We will discover other things as well, for which we must be prepared. But we cannot ascend K'nath until we have cleansed ourselves within the Murmuring Pool, and that is some little ways away. Let us proceed out of this haunted woodland onto the moonlit roadway."

They stalked among the bending trees, past the bristling bushes that tried to trip them, until they reached the winding road. Rebecca stopped and lifted her face to the midnight sky.

"What have you done to the moonlight, Edgar?"

"Madame?"

"That globe has lost its pearly luster, and one imagines that its light might soon be extinguished. And your face—that milky countenance—seems much brighter than when first we encountered you. Yours is a lunatic wizardry indeed, if the texture of your dreamland flesh is supping on the moon's radiance and thus depleting the pale patina of that globe."

"If I am the stuff of dreams, so is that spectral sphere of dust, which has no illumination except that which it usurps from other sources. Perhaps it has taught me that trick of appropriation, and thus I gleam more boldly than before." The poet leaned nearer to the film actress and studied her in silence for a little while. "But we share a common taint, my lady; for neither of us exist as concrete things in the waking world. We are, in that realm, dust returned unto dust, and although we have assumed our former semblances, we are no more than shadows." He slid his eyes away from hers and glanced at Agnes. "Hers is a different tale altogether."

"She is no concern of yours, sirrah," she sighed quietly. And then she raised her voice and said, "Let us continue, and worm ourselves along this ancient way."

Agnes smiled as she overheard the softly spoken exchange, and she walked ahead of the others with an assured step. She could feel a kind of vibrancy blossoming within her, a latent power that, with arcane exercise, would flower into witchcraft of her own design. Not glancing back to see if the others followed, Agnes wandered along the roadway nonchalantly. Now and then she saw the distant stars that dislodged from heaven and fell toward the surface of dreamland, and she envied those stars their flight; and so she concentrated on summoning a windstorm, and as the mild tempest tangled her hair and twisted the folds of her gown, she stepped onto it and walked upon the wind, ignoring the shouting that commenced behind her. Floating two feet above the dirt road, she sailed along to where the woodland ended and there was naught but open ground and vibrantly green grass. Agnes rushed through the air until she espied a coil of smoke rising from a chimney, and stepping from the wind, she walked along the smooth roadway until coming to a small clutch of cottages along the wayside. The door of the cottage nearest her was open, and Agnes listened to a whirring sound that whispered from within. Silently, she stepped to the door and then crossed the threshold; and she was greeted by the smiling face of a gentleman at a Saxony spinning wheel, whose eyes sparkled magically in the dimly lit room.

"Your dress is just there," he told her, nodding his head toward a chair in one corner of the room, over which a gown of black fabric was draped. "The alcove just over there can serve as changing room. Don't become alarmed if the material seems to cling to you at first— it needs to adapt to the texture of your pseudo−flesh."

Her "pseudo−flesh"—the phrase made Agnes momentarily contemplate the nature of her dreamland self, and how removed it was from her dreaming material self in the waking world. Embracing herself, she could feel a mass of flesh that seemed to be of physical matter. Had she crossed the threshold of dream in her body of flesh and bone, or was the physicality she now seemed to experience merely a dreamland trick? Was it Simon's actual form that had been swept away in the river's rushing water; or did he recline, slumbering yet very real, somewhere in Sesqua Valley?

Walking to the ebony gown, she ran her fingers over its smooth material and sighed with a kind of sensual pleasure at its softness. Not bothering to step into the dressing alcove, Agnes removed her clothing and slipped into this new apparel, the fabric of which did indeed cling to her form so that her handsome figure was exhibited. Hearing a sound, she looked at the doorway, where her companions stood gaping at her. Looking to the spinning wheel, Agnes saw that the fellow sitting at it had vanished.

"You look very handsome, Agnes," Rebecca told her. "But come—we must to the pool."

Without speaking a word in response, the young woman walked to her attendant and passed through the cottage's threshold.

Chapter XXI

Mandy and Penelope departed the Weird Tales Museum and started walking north through a succession of squalid commercial zones and then a series of dilapidated residential districts toward a distant imposing mountain with a double peak that lay in the wildness beyond the boundaries of Dylath—Leen.

"Have you eaten anything today, dear?" asked Penelope. "Personally, I had a light breakfast, but that was hours ago and this exercise has giving me quite an appetite."

"Not a thing," the girl answered. That's how Penelope thought of Mandy: as a girl—child. Even though she knew Mandy was a fully grown woman in the waking world, her present extremely youthful appearance argued against thinking of her as such. "I traveled all night and arrived in the city at dawn but didn't want to risk missing you, so I stationed myself in the editor's office early this morning and had no opportunity to find any food."

Penelope stopped abruptly and pointed at a small two—story wooden house across the street that had been converted into a quaint restaurant. She was favorably impressed by the fact that not only had it been painted recently, but the rose garden in the front yard was well tended.

"Let's go in that charming—looking café and see what they offer in the way of lunch."

"Sure. This is a good place to stop. We're in no particular hurry, other than wanting to get Jimmy back as soon as possible. We can take a break."

"Lunch it is."

Penelope's initial good impression of the little café was bolstered when she saw how clean and tidy it was inside. Perhaps being located somewhat inland, a mile or two from the waterfront, allowed it to attract a more reputable clientele than did the seedy taverns and fish houses that festered on the docks. The interior décor further encouraged her. Cheerful, fluffy white curtains trimmed the windows, and the small tables in the dining room were adorned with red and white checkerboard tablecloths, not to mention gleaming brass oil lamps and chrome dispensers full of napkins.

"Yes," said the older woman, "this will do quite nicely."

They weren't seated more than a minute when a neatly groomed, dark-haired gentleman with a spotless white apron tied around his narrow waist came out and handed them each a large menu.

"Welcome to Café Loveman, ladies. Can I get you anything to drink while you're looking over the menu?"

"By any wild stretch of the imagination, do you have green tea?"

"But of course, madame."

"Wonderful! I'll have a cup, hot. How about you, Mandy?"

"Water's fine for me."

"You're sure? We may not find an establishment that serves tea again in this dreadfully uncivilized outpost."

"No, thanks. Water's perfect."

"As you please, miss."

The waiter, whom for some reason Penelope assumed was also the owner as well as the cook, dashed off and returned a moment later with a pot of hot water and a china teacup in which rested a tea bag. He placed these carefully before Penelope. Another quick dash into the kitchen and he returned with a glass of ice water for Mandy.

"I'll give you a few minutes to decide, ladies," he said, bowing graciously.

"Well," said Penelope to Mandy, "I've just found my favorite restaurant in Dylath-Leen. I give it four stars on the service alone. If the food is edible, five stars."

Mandy smiled at Penelope's dry wit.

"So what's the plan, my dear?" asked Penelope as she poured hot water into her cup and then lifted the tea bag by its string and let it fall several times in a row so as to speed up the steeping process.

Mandy took a leisurely sip of water, closing her eyes so as to savor its refreshing qualities to the full. Setting the glass back down, she replied, "There's a derelict old mansion on the side of that mountain to our north. Once we've eaten, we'll make our way there. I believe we may find in that mansion a means by which we may pass from this realm and into the dreamland of witchery."

"Will we be traveling by land, air, or sea?"

"By magick."

"*Magick?* Oh, my." Penelope frowned in disapproval. She had no patience for anything associated with the New Age movement. Every time she heard the word "magick" it raised her hackles. "I hadn't considered that possibility."

"It's much faster, Penelope, and we'll avoid the many discomforts of extended travel by conventional methods."

"Are you sure it's safe?"

"No, not entirely—but then, what is, really?"

"True enough." Turning her attention to the menu, Penelope decided on a patty melt on rye and the *soup du jour,* which happened to be cream of broccoli, one of her favorites, while Mandy picked the baked potato with sour cream and chives. The proprietor, who according to his name badge was Mr. Loveman himself, took their order, assuring the ladies that they'd both made excellent choices and would not be disappointed.

Penelope was three bites into her patty melt when she realized they were not alone in the dining room. Something unusual caught her eye, and when she looked in the direction of a lone table set far back into the shadows at the opposite corner of the room, she noticed what appeared to be a vague, insubstantial figure lingering there, seated, with no meal set before it. The entity was dark, its features difficult to distinguish, and it had an annoying habit of flickering in an almost supernatural way, being halfway transparent at times, fully solid at other moments, and completely invisible still other moments, as if the thing were only partially there. Penelope detected something decidedly ghastly about the motionless entity. To her mind, it greatly resembled a decomposing corpse, one lately retrieved from its casket still garbed in the ragged, deteriorating man's suit that had served as its burial shroud.

"Are you seeing what I'm seeing?" Penelope whispered, nodding toward the mysterious apparition.

"Pay it no mind," said Mandy matter-of-factly. "That's the disembodied spirit of the graduate student who's been stalking me these past few weeks. What's his name? Charles. Right now his body is sound asleep in his rented room in Arkham, dreaming a rather conventional dream where he's in the Hobo Bean coffee shop between classes, leering at me in his gross way and trying to get me to pay attention to him. Before he went to bed, he performed an occult ritual that he hoped would transport him here to dreamland, where he imagines he could somehow get together with me romantically—for he rather accurately believes that I spend half my time in dreamland and the other half in the mundane waking world. But the sad truth is that he doesn't have the metaphysical power to get here fully on his own, and in fact he's not really here at all. He's only *partially* here, alternating between dreamland and the waking world. That's what causes that peculiar flickering effect you see. He's oscillating between the two dimensions, not firmly ensconced in either one. And he is not at all aware of the fact that he's only halfway anchored in dreamland. He doesn't perceive this delightful café we sit in; to him it's the coffee shop back home. This rude distraction will last about a minute more and then he'll be gone, his spirit yanked back to a regular dream state in the mundane world. Ignore him. He can't see you at all, and he really can't even see me as I truly am. All he sees is his fantasized image of what I would look like if I were there with him in his dreamed coffee shop, making eyes at him. Poor fool."

"Heavens, this is a baffling place. I'm glad you understand it, my dear."

"Apparently, I understand it as well as I do because when I'm here—I have discovered—I feel as if I've *always* been here, although, in the conventional time frame of the waking world, we are both relative newcomers in dreamland. That's something you'll get used to; the waking world and dreamland are on radically different time tracks. There's no chronological interrelationship between the two realms. Something that happened long ago in dreamland may have happened yesterday in the waking world. Likewise, something that hasn't happened yet in dreamland already happened in the waking world. It's very confusing at first, but you'll catch on after a while."

"I see. That *will* take some getting used to. Oh well, I'm always game for learning new things."

Just as Mandy promised, the bilocating specter of Charles Mo-relle weakly flickered a few times more in sputtering bursts and then faded from view, leaving behind only a wispy blue fog that shim-mered in the air before it evaporated into nothingness.

"See, I told you," said Mandy with a big smile.

"Amazing. Glad that's over," said Penelope, eyeing the bill that had just been laid before her.

The entire meal cost them only twenty cents and was not only edible but delicious. Penelope paid with a pair of worn dimes she took from a coin purse that was in the pocket of the shift she'd taken from the hotel closet that morning, including an extra nickel as a tip for Mr. Loveman. Then they were on their way again.

By late afternoon, still journeying on foot, they had reached the edge of town where a run—down funicular trolley station bloomed like an exotic weed in a dirt lot at the end of the last residential street in Dylath—Leen.

Chapter XXII

The trolley station was nestled at the base of a tall mountain situated on Dylath—Leen's city limits. It occupied a small portion of a sprawl—ing dirt lot that bordered the town's northern most neighborhood. The station consisted of a ticket booth, a boarding platform, and two parallel rail tracks that ran side by side up the steep mountainside.

"It's electrically powered," observed Mandy. "There's a pulley system, with two counterbalanced cars running on separate tracks. The gravitational pull upon the descending car on one side helps lift the ascending car on the other side. The cars cross paths in the mid—dle, exactly halfway up the mountain. It's beautifully balanced."

"Very clever," said Penelope. "When I was a little girl," she suddenly, somewhat inappropriately, reminisced, "I rode on a fu—nicular train with my father, during a trip to Los Angeles. It was known as the Angel's Flight Railway, and it was in a strange little neighborhood called Bunker Hill. Being an innocent child, I thought the train would actually take us high enough up in the air to see some real angels. It was rather disappointing because all we saw were some sad—looking prostitutes sitting on window sills in a crummy apartment building on the side of the hill. They were all eating or—anges, for heaven's sake. They were hardly angels, let me tell you."

"I wouldn't be too sure of that," replied Mandy, with a knowing smile.

Penelope stared at her in disbelief, not a little shocked at what Mandy was implying, but she said nothing. Instead, she changed the subject. "Let's buy our tickets before they sell out." A sizable crowd had formed at the ticket window, and they fell into place at the end of the line.

"It's the usual weekday afternoon rush," said Mandy. "Everyone is headed home after their day's activities in the city."

"How late does the trolley run?"

"Until 6 P.M. After that, if you want to come up or down, your only option is the road, which is very steep and perilous. The trolley is much safer."

"So I take it we're not planning a trip back down tonight?"

"Most likely not."

According to the fares hand−painted on a weathered plywood sign beside the ticket window, it would cost them a nickel each to ride one way. Penelope dug around in her coin purse and came up with two five−cent pieces from 1918 featuring the image of a buffalo on one side and the head of an American Indian, complete with feathered headdress, on the other.

"The PC crowd back home would have a fit over this," she mumbled, examining the portraits.

"Hmm?"

"Oh, nothing." She placed the coins on the counter and the burly man behind the window slid two tickets toward her.

"Let's find good seats before it fills up," advised Penelope.

"I'd like an end seat so I can watch the scenery."

"That you shall have, my dear."

While they had been waiting in line, the light had shifted from the warm, golden radiance of late afternoon to a deep crimson tint that made the skyline appear to be bathed in blood—an effect made even more ominous by the mysterious purple shadows clinging to the cre−vasses and recesses of the mountain. Not daring to hesitate, Mandy and Penelope claimed a suitable pair of seats in the lead car, and in short order the rest of the seats around and behind them filled in with pas−sengers. Then two men wearing railway uniforms appeared. One was the motorman, his role made obvious when he took his position at the controls. The other was the conductor, who promptly went to work collecting the tickets that had just been handed out moments ago.

"Oh, brother," Penelope complained, "they give you a ticket and then they take it away."

"I wonder what they do with them all?" asked Mandy.

"Probably turn around and sell them to the next load of idiots going up the hill."

Mandy pressed her lips together and tapped at them with her forefinger. After a moment of introspection, she said, "No, I think not. The answer is that after they're collected, the tickets are shipped off in big bundles to a remote desert land where they are released in midair by a giant bird flying high overhead, and the tickets come fluttering down like leaves falling on the plain. All the tickets collected from all the passengers on all the trains and trolleys and buses in the entire world including the dreamlands are deposited on that desolate plain—so many tickets that they litter the ground in every direction, from horizon to horizon. When they first arrive in that realm, travelers stop and pick up a few of the tickets, but when they look about and see there are no trains or trolleys or buses anywhere to be found, well, they realize the tickets are useless and let them fall from their hands, to be trod upon by future travelers as they sojourn across a sea of littered paper."

From Penelope's expression, it was clear she considered the girl to be mad as a hatter. "That's quite poetic, my dear, but you know it can't possibly be true."

"Oh, it's true, Penelope. Anything we imagine is true in the dreamlands."

"If you insist."

With all the passengers seated and the boarding platform cleared, the motorman pulled the throttle, powerful motors groaned, and the trolley lurched forward with a series of metallic clunks and began its spasmodic climb up the hill.

Penelope glanced over at an elderly gentleman in the seat beside her. He was attired in a neatly pressed Victorian frock coat and top hat. From an inner pocket he extracted a paperbound volume and began to read, moving his lips silently as he scanned the pages. Staring at the lurid cover a little more intently than she considered po−

lite, Penelope was able to make out the book's title: *Sunset Terrace Thriller: An Erotic Entertainment.*

Indeed! she mused. *The old coot couldn't wait until he was behind closed doors to indulge his disgusting literary perversion.* Something about that title made her feel disturbed, offended, and unworldly all at the same time.

As the train labored upward, they passed a number of quaint gardens, most of which were visible only for a few seconds, being largely concealed by the lush vegetation of the hillside. Penelope noted the prevalence of classically themed sculptures adorning these gardens: fauns playing pipes, cherub boys urinating in fountains, Pan being indecent with a goat, Aphrodite modestly attempting to cover herself. There was something decidedly unseemly about these artworks. Just as she was adjusting to that unpleasantness, one of the Pan figures—remarkably—moved, lifting an arm to wave languidly, and then turning its head until the thing's white marble eyes locked onto hers.

"Good heavens, Mandy! That statue is alive!"

Mandy turned to see, but by then the animate Pan and the garden he occupied were no longer in view.

"Sorry, I didn't catch it, Penny. But I do believe you. Remember: this place is not like the waking world. Different rules apply here, or no rules at all. Whatever happens just seems to happen."

"I can see that's the case. What next? One dare not even imagine the potential horrors of this godforsaken place, lest they are visited upon us."

"That would be wise."

In due time the trolley reached its summit, which was approximately halfway up the mountainside, and came to a halt at the upper boarding platform. The majority of disembarking passengers walked a short distance laterally down a cobblestone road to the cluster of homes where most of the locals lived. A handful of others—Penelope and Mandy among them—took a narrower footpath leading to the few homes positioned at higher levels on the mountain.

"We're almost there," Mandy assured Penelope, noting that the older woman was beginning to look exhausted. "With any luck, we'll get a bite to eat and a comfortable bed before we set off on the next leg of our journey."

"One can only hope," Penelope said with all the stoicism she could muster.

By now the sun had completely set, leaving behind a band of scarlet radiance adhering to the horizon.

"The view from up here's really beautiful, don't you think?" asked Mandy. "With the city spread out below, its lights twinkling. Quite a vantage point, I'd say."

"Indeed, it's a pretty sight, were I in any mood for gawking at sunsets."

They proceeded in silence. One passenger after another peeled off onto side paths, ultimately leaving only the two of them winding their way toward their destination, with Mandy in the lead and an increasingly anxious Penelope following. The soft glow of the flash-lights carried by many of the passengers down their respective paths gave them the appearance of fireflies flitting through the woods this way and that, an illusion that added to the mood of mystery quietly overcoming both women. Penelope and Mandy came to a clearing in the foliage, and an old ruin of a mansion reared into view. They passed through the unlocked gates of a tall brick fence surrounding the mansion and followed a fern−lined walkway toward the entrance of the imposing structure.

"We're in luck!" exclaimed Mandy. "There's a light in the win-dow. Someone's there to greet us!"

"Or slit our throats as a fine ending for a miserable day," grum-bled Penelope.

"Oh, it hasn't been all that bad, has it? We've had some fun to-day, haven't we?"

"I suppose we have."

And with that grudging admission from Penelope, Mandy knocked with the heavy iron knocker on the huge wooden door, and they waited for the arrival of whoever or whatever might answer their solicitation.

CHAPTER XXIII

A full two minutes elapsed after Mandy knocked on the door of the ancient mansion, and still no one answered.

"Perhaps they're out for the evening," suggested Penelope.

"I doubt it. I was told we would be granted admission. We are expected."

She rapped again with the oversized cast–iron knocker fashioned in the image of an elongated demon's head.

"Coming!" called out a muffled masculine voice from within. A moment later there was the metallic sound of locks being unlocked and bolts sliding, and the door swung open on its creaky hinges. A servant in livery stood before them with no detectable expression on his drawn–out face.

"Good evening, ladies," he said in a monotone. "Kindly follow me." The man, who was bald, frightfully thin, and looked to be in his mid–sixties, led Penelope and Mandy through a dark foyer and into a dimly illuminated drawing room. With a flourish of his hand toward a group of overstuffed chairs, he indicated they should seat themselves. "I will announce your arrival," he said, bowing politely before making his exit.

"Who exactly is it we're seeing?" asked Penelope a little nerv–ously.

"I wasn't given a name," answered Mandy in a half–whisper. "He's an influential figure in this community who can facilitate our passage to the place where James is being held. That's all I really know."

"So we are taking it on faith that these are reputable people who will do us no harm?"

"Yes, they will not harm us and they're ready to help, although I don't know about the reputable part. I was told we can definitely trust them, at least in this matter. We're safe in their hands."

"I certainly hope so . . ."

Still seated with her hands grasping her knees through the fabric of the plain cotton shift and with her back arched, Penelope gazed around the room, bored at having to wait. The décor was far too lavish for a woman of her simple tastes: red velvet paper lining the walls, an abundance of small oil paintings and nineteenth-century albumen photo prints in ornate gilded frames, and several pieces of heavy rosewood furniture bearing highly polished surfaces.

"It's a bit much, don't you think?" she said, her eyes darting around to indicate she was referring to their surroundings.

"Fancy indeed," said Mandy in an effort to agree in a non-judgmental way.

"I was thinking more 'gaudy' than 'fancy.'"

"Oh, I think it's lovely, especially when one considers the squalor we witnessed down by the waterfront."

"True. I'd rather spend the evening here than in one of those dives we passed earlier today."

A crowded bookcase on the opposite wall caught Penelope's attention. She rose, crossed the room, and pulled a volume bound in blue Moroccan leather from the shelf. Turning to the front matter, she read aloud the title: *"A Universal History of Yearning,"*

"What a curious title," observed Mandy.

"It sounds like smutty writing to me," Penelope declared.

"Maybe not. Maybe it's a sad book, a melancholy tale of wistful yearning for a lost loved one. It might be a tender expression of the deepest secrets of the human heart."

"No, I'm sure it must be vile trash, my dear. These male authors take every good thing in life and distort it to the service of their lust. They turn their wives into whores and their whores into carnal beasts. It's an ugly world out there, Mandy."

"You think so?"

"I know so."

"Well, even if it is that kind of literature, you have to admit it's still a beautiful book, physically. The fine leather and gold tooling—it's a work of art, really."

"Lipstick on a pig, my dear." Penelope slid the book back into its place in the bookcase. At that moment, the sound of laughter came to her from behind a pair of crimson curtains hanging to her right. Parting the curtains, she discovered behind them a pair of French doors leading to an outside balcony where two figures appeared in silhouette. Although no one had invited her out there and she knew she might be imposing, Penelope opened the doors and stepped out onto the balcony, where she was bathed in the pale blue light of a waxing moon.

Coming closer, she saw that the figures were two men huddled in wicker chairs, conversing in low tones, their backs turned to her. Both wore dark blue railway jackets and caps; she suspected they must be the conductor and motorman who earlier had taken her and Mandy up the hillside on the funicular trolley. Now, their day's work done, they were relaxing, having a drink and smoking while engaging in a bit of harmless banter. Surely they wouldn't mind her interrupting for a moment to thank them for their service. The fellow on the left, who was not quite as portly as his companion, looked like the motorman. From her seat behind him on the trolley, she had seen his face from time to time during their trip up, but not wanting him to think she was staring, she had avoided making eye contact. Now, she was pretty sure it was him, although his face was not currently visible.

"Good evening, gentlemen. I was one of your passengers on the last trip up. I just want to thank you—" began Penelope, but she didn't get to finish this pleasantry because at that moment both men rose from their chairs and turned around to face her, and she saw that each man held a whiskey glass in one hand and a cigar in the other. That was not unusual. What was highly unusual was the fact that on each man the body part that normally would be called a face was a largely featureless ovoid, other than having a mouth complete with tongue and teeth. These bizarre entities lacked any semblance of a nose, eyes, brow, facial hair, or any other feature you would expect to find on a human being. They were, simply put, faceless monsters.

Hardly aware that she was gasping in horror, Penelope backed out through the French doors, closing them after her, pulled the crimson curtains tightly shut, and silently returned to her chair to wait for the master of the house.

"Who were you speaking with just now on the balcony?" asked Mandy.

"The conductor and motorman from the trolley," said Penelope, feeling much too weary to describe to Mandy the unfathomable horror of the faceless men.

"Oh, how very pleasant. They must be acquaintances of whoever owns this home."

"Apparently so."

"And how are they doing this evening?"

"Just peachy. We had a lovely chat. I do wish the master of the house would get here. I'm rather tired of waiting for him, and we both could use a meal, assuming he intends to offer us dinner."

"Oh, yes," agreed Mandy, "I'm quite famished. That was a light lunch I had at the Café Loveman and we've been very active. I've worked up a good appetite, as I'm sure you have, too."

"I could eat a proverbial horse," Penelope stated emphatically.

They heard the muffled sound of footsteps on carpeting, and seconds later the servant who had let them in reappeared. He nodded in what might be interpreted as a half-hearted bow, closing his eyes in a not quite sincere display of deference while tilting his head to one side.

"If you will be so kind as to follow me, ladies, the master will receive you now."

"Splendid," exclaimed Penelope, practically leaping forward. The women followed the servant down a hallway that was dimly lit by torchières mounted on the wall to their left, and ending in an arched doorway that opened unto a pitch-black room of unknown dimensions.

"Someone forgot to buy light bulbs," grumbled Penelope.

"Really?" asked Mandy.

"I'm joking, dear, although you do have to wonder."

Arriving at the threshold of the room, the servant positioned himself beside the door frame and, with an extravagant flourish, invited the ladies to step in.

"Is there a wall switch?" Penelope inquired.

"Please, bear with us, madame. My master prefers it this way."

"Oh, certainly. We wouldn't want to put him out in any way." She took a couple of baby steps inside, sensing that Mandy was directly behind her.

"Hello?" Penelope spoke into the ebon void, turning this way and that, although it was utterly hopeless; the blackness was impenetrable and there was virtually nothing to be seen.

"Good evening, ladies, and welcome," came a somber voice from deep within the Stygian gloom.

"Oh. There is someone here after all. How lovely," answered Penelope snidely. "Shall we come in, or are you coming out?"

"Please enter. It's entirely safe, I assure you."

"If you insist, although if I bump into a table and break a lamp, I'm not going to feel terribly responsible, given the situation."

"Just a bit further," said the male voice, which sounded quite elderly.

Penelope took another step, sensing that Mandy was right behind her.

"How's this, sir?" Penelope asked.

"That's perfect."

Hearing that his master was satisfied, the servant produced a metal canister from the pocket of his coat, unscrewed the lid, and, raising it high, released an eclipse of moths into the air. The insects, momentarily confused, quickly assembled into a swarm and flew toward the spot whence the master's voice had issued. Penelope was startled to see they were luminous, emitting a pale white light. The creatures at first landed upon the hidden man's face, thus revealing the contours of his nose, cheeks, eye sockets, and other aspects of his physiognomy, then coated his neck and shoulders, flowed down on—to his chest, abdomen, and pelvis, and finally alighted upon his legs and feet, so that the man was evoked not by the play of light on his actual being, but through the secondary medium of glimmering insects.

"How wonderful! The moths have made it so we can see you," said Mandy.

"It is highly unusual, I'll grant you that," chimed in Penelope.

"You are much too kind, dear ladies. While I fear this unusual means of making an appearance before my guests without actually venturing into the light may seem ridiculous or even ostentatious, it really is a matter of practicality, for I am a creature of darkness and my mortal frame must remain occluded under the arcane laws that govern my being. Exposure to even the dimmest rays of light would not only be incredibly painful for me, but would endanger my health and might very well prove fatal."

"Heavens!" exclaimed Penelope, sounding both startled and sincerely concerned. "Do you mean to say that the light would literally kill you? I've never heard of such a thing. Is it a rare medical condition?"

"No, it's a common spiritual condition, but let us not dwell on my infirmities. I am content enough to linger in the shadows, covered by these innocent glowing insects. As you can surmise, I am in no condition to join you for dinner, but I do not intend for you to go hungry under my roof. If you'll kindly follow my man, he'll escort you to the kitchen where my cook has prepared a meal for you, and after that there are comfortable bedchambers where you may refresh yourself and rest until midnight, for surely you are tired after your long journey."

"We are indeed both hungry and tired, good sir," replied Penelope. "Thank you for your kindness and hospitality."

"And what happens at midnight?" asked Mandy.

"Ah," answered the voice that issued from the moth—covered figure. "Midnight is when more guests arrive, and with their assistance you both will be transported to the land of your brother's im—

prisonment." And with that, the strange ancient man with the thin, dry voice bid them a good evening, and then violently shook him‐ self, causing the moths to scatter in all directions, leaving him again entirely invisible, a void amidst blackness.

CHAPTER XXIV

Unlike the opulence of the other rooms that Mandy and Penelope had visited in the mansion, the kitchen was humble and utilitarian. The cook gave them each a bowl of stew and then turned her back on them and went about her chores in silence. Penelope was grateful for that, as she was tired and preferred not to engage in conversation. Just as they finished their meal, the male servant reappeared to escort them to their bedrooms upstairs. He led them to an adjacent suite of rooms, explaining that he would call on them at a quarter–hour before twelve, so they would have a few minutes to prepare for what he called "the event."

"Which is exactly, what, if I may inquire?" asked Penelope.

"Well, it's my understanding that you will be attending a séance at midnight, in this very house, to which certain guests have been invited, although I can reveal no more than that at this time. The Master enjoys his share of drama."

"I see. Very well. A séance, is it? And you'll wake us in time? We've come a long distance and don't want to miss anything."

"Indeed, I shall rap lightly on your chamber door to rouse you."

"Excellent, thank you, sir."

Alone in her room, Penelope lay down on the bed on top of the covers, fully dressed, and closed her eyes, intending only to rest and not to sleep, for there was something about the house and its eccentric owner that gave her an unsettled feeling. But despite her intent, she must have fallen into a dream, for the next thing she knew she was standing at the French doors, looking out upon the room's bal–

cony. And there, in a dreamy wash of deep blue moon–glow, she saw a face from her past that filled her with a tender longing. It was someone she had not seen since she was a young woman on the very threshold of her life. He was a young man, just a boy really, whom she had loved very much and had been forced to part with. He looked exactly as he had all those years ago, not having aged even a little. She reached out her hand and, extending it through the open doors, gently touched his face, and in return he smiled. Then she turned and saw herself—young and almost beautiful again in that fierce way she had had back then—reflected in the mottled antique mirror across the room, and her heart was glad.

As promised, the servant gave a series of restrained knocks on the door, awakening Penelope from the unexpected sweetness of the dream. Acknowledging him, she rose from the bed, smoothed the wrinkles in her shift, and arranged her hair as best she could with her fingers, having no brush, while staring at her image in the same mir–ror that now showed her as the aging woman she was. She was ready for the séance.

Chapter XXV

The small group exited the building and stood for a moment just before it as Edgar, trembling slightly, lifted his face to the azure-tinted moon that hovered high above the church. "Let me pause one moment and drink the exquisite moon," he sighed.

"How wonderful," cooed Rebecca, "that Luna should so resemble the sphere humanity calls Neptune—a planet that is linked to dream, shadow, and the occult. Indeed, perhaps that isn't the moon that casts its chilly light upon us, but the eighth planet from our sun of temporary fire."

Bending to the ground, she touched a spot of dirt where grass did not grow, dug one finger into that sod, and began to etch a symbol that resembled a kind of pitchfork. Agnes recognized it as the astronomical symbol for Neptune, and yet the way that Rebecca etched it, the symbol took on an evil aspect, reminding the younger woman of a Devil's Trident. A wind arose, from some deep place in the woods, and began to moan as it moved past the slightly swaying trees. Rising, Rebecca faced the wind and parted her lips, as if to feast on some essence of the gale. As they watched, the woman's face began to alter and its color began to fade. The actress closed her eyes for some few seconds, and when she opened them again their surface was entirely black, making it appear that her sockets were void of occupants. And then a portion of lunar light began to blossom where her eyes had once been, and her orbs appeared as spools of silver. They watched, and it seemed that drops of crimson were being spilled onto the centers of the silver orbs. She turned solemnly and regarded them with eyes composed of blood and moonlight. "It's time to leave this woodland."

As her voice issued from between her lips, it was accompanied by a mauve—tinted mist that floated to Agnes, who inhaled a portion of it with her nostrils and felt the effluvium seep upward, where it coiled behind her eyes. Some cold presence entered her head and, rising, chilled her brain. For a moment, her vision clouded and her senses became numb, and she imagined that she herself was being transformed into a semblance of fog that filtered forward through the moonlit aether. But then a snapping sound assaulted her, and she awakened as if from dreaming to find that she had stepped onto a thick twig as she moved through the woodland, following Rebecca.

They escaped the woods, but not the moonlight. More and more, Agnes could feel that sphere's icy illumination on her eyes; and as her eyes grew glacial, the scene that they drank in began to change. Minute particles of what might have been frost floated be—fore her in the air, resembling dusts motes scattered in the air that are revealed in shafts of sunlight. The night's sky, as she raised her eyes to observe it, took on a pale mauve tint. As she studied that sky, the young woman shuddered. She watched the queer slate clouds that drifted to the moon and conjoined with it, so that the moon became a distorted daemon in her view. And then two points of red fire peered into her eyes, burning into her brain. The frost—daemon that had taken hold of Agnes melted away as she gazed into the ignited eyes of Rebecca Pascal.

"Your gifts of witchery continue to grow, young woman. And yet they are unruly, and you may yet become their pawn. Monsters may be evoked by instinct, unconsciously and without ceremony. You must be cautious of such influences, if you are to be a Mistress of dark craft. Be in control of the wonders of which this dreamland can instruct you. Do not become their manipulated puppet."

"This alchemy is intoxicating," Agnes responded, hugging herself as her eyes sparkled with a kind of fire all their own. "I feel over—whelmed by influence!"

"Come, we are near the garden of the murmuring pool. Drink—

ing of the water there will wash unwanted voices from your mind, and your self-control will become assured. Come."

Agnes felt slightly unsteady and lifted her hand to her face, the flesh of which felt alien. She then saw Edgar's small soft hand sail through the air to hers, which he clasped, brought to his lips and kissed. Hand in hand, the couple followed Rebecca through the night, across a field and to a tiny dreamland hamlet. In the center of the village, they found an enclosed garden surrounded by rose hedges. They entered the enclosed area, and Agnes imagined that the night became subtly brighter, that the foreboding, bewitched atmosphere lightened so as to lose some particles of gloom. Agnes listened to what sounded like a continuous susurration that advanced from a sunken pool at the center of the garden.

Edgar stepped to the pool and knelt before it. Its water was unclear and slightly frothy, and an odor that reminded the poet of talc issued from the liquid. "What is this spectral babble that infuses the purple air? See there, that cherub face that almost forms beneath the foam, huddled there among those indistinct white stones. See its pale and squelchy orbs, those eyes that seem to be composed of tears. There—there! It rises and takes on solid form!"

Feeling a presence beside him, Edgar looked up at Rebecca and watched as she held out her hand. The ghostly sphere that looked so like some ethereal amoretto floated to the outstretched hand, and then stopped just before its fingers. Edgar watched those fingers move in an esoteric way as the murmuring from the pool increased in volume, and when he gazed again into the liquid depths he saw that what he had mistaken for white stones were childlike faces, immaterial and fantastic, that rose up and broke through the surface of water. These phantom physiognomies floated over the heads of the human congregation, putting out the starlight with the filmy breath from their pale faces. Rebecca took hold of the countenance before her and, turning it, attached it to her face as if it were a fairy mask; and then she stalked to where Agnes stood and pressed both of her hands on the younger woman's shoulder. Agnes knelt, keeping her eyes on the eerie orbs of the angelic face that regarded her.

"You possess the gift of innocence," the face informed her, in a voice that contained numerous tones. "There is great power in such virtuousness, especially in a world as corrupt as this. We welcome your purity of soul, and enforce it." Rebecca's body tilted slightly forward as the seraphic visage stretched wide its mouth. A stream of sparkling water spilled from that mouth and bathed the mortal's head. Trembling and weeping softly, Agnes clasped her sodden face with both hands and washed the liquid into the texture of her skin. Aspects of light and darkness began to spin around her, and she became dizzy as she watched them, until at last her vision darkened and she felt her body fall onto the ground.

CHAPTER XXVI

Mandy failed to respond when the servant repeatedly knocked on her bedroom door in a series of what began as mild taps but quickly grew in intensity until they became fairly insistent raps. Impatient with his excessive deference when it came to dealing with feminine visitors to the household, Penelope brushed past the man and barged into Mandy's guest room, finding the girl curled up in a fetal position on the bed, deep in the thrall of slumber. Not hesitating in the least, she went straight to Mandy and grabbed her by the shoulder, giving a good shake while loudly commanding, "You must get up, dear. It's time for our séance!"

Still groggy, her eyes crisped with sleep and her hair unruly, Mandy lethargically followed Penelope and the servant up a flight of stairs to a small room on the third floor where the session was about to begin. As had been the case with Penelope, there was no need for Mandy to dress first as she'd slept in her clothes, having been too exhausted to change into the nightgown that had been so thought-fully laid out for her by the help.

The servant announced the two women by name, and with some trepidation they entered the room where a number of people were assembled around a circular table. Penelope recognized each of them as individuals she had already encountered in other settings during her brief time in this strange realm. At the right side of the table sat the Enchantress whom Penelope had met the night she had gone walking alone on the beach. This was the same woman who had promised Penelope that somebody would help her find her little brother, and now here she was, at the séance where something or other was supposed to happen that would lead to the hoped—for re—union with James. Seated to the Enchantress's right on the far side of the table was the dark—haired gentleman who had served them lunch at Café Loveman earlier that day, and to his right sat the gypsy woman who had told her fortune in the hotel lobby that morning. Next to the gypsy were two empty chairs, with a third one posi—tioned on the left side of the table and then two more empty chairs on the near side of the table immediately in front of Penelope and Mandy. Of all people who should happen to be at the gathering, the most surprising to Penelope were the motorman and conductor from the trolley that had brought them up the mountainside to this aged mansion. These two mysterious men—if indeed men they be—stood solemnly behind the table holding elongated candles that provided the room's only illumination. As before, their faces were hideously smooth, featureless blobs of pasty flesh, except for their mouths, which bore what looked to Penelope like knowing smirks.

The two empty chairs closest to them were apparently intended for Mandy and Penelope. She couldn't imagine who might be sitting in the three other vacant chairs, if anyone.

"Don't be shy, my dears," said the Enchantress. "Have a seat and we'll promptly get started." In an aside to Penelope she whispered, "I see you solved my little riddle about the room where it is always sunset. Very clever of you, but I expected nothing less."

Penelope was the first to be seated, choosing the chair on her right, the one closest to the Enchantress. Creepy as she was, Penelo—pe trusted this ridiculous woman with all her occult affectations more than she did the gaudily dressed gypsy hag whom she would have been sitting closer to, had she taken the chair on the left. Mandy, who appeared to be fully awake now, took the chair next to Penelope.

"Ah!" said the gypsy woman, nodding knowingly first toward Penelope and then toward Mandy. "It is as I predicted when the cards were dealt and you revealed the secrets of your heart. You have entered into a blessed partnership with the enlightened one—the girl who is kind and wise beyond her years. This bodes well for your ul—

timate success in the venture you have undertaken."

"You mean Miss Mandy here?" Penelope asked. "Well, yes, she is proving to be a good guide through this unfathomable place. And she's quite easy to get along with. I do enjoy her company. But, honestly, I have no idea what you're talking about, madame."

"No matter," replied the gypsy, reaching across the table and patting Penelope's hand comfortingly. "All is well."

"Do not condescend to me," Penelope mumbled under her breath.

"Very pleasant to see you again, ladies," blurted out Loveman with considerable hesitancy, fearing that he might be imposing. "I trust you've had your supper?"

"We have, Mr. Loveman, thank you for asking," said Mandy. "We ate right here—well, downstairs, in the kitchen. The master of the house saw to it that we were given a very yummy meal."

"And what, if may I inquire, were you served?"

"We had stew! A beef stew with potatoes and vegetables. Also carrots, celery, onions, and some greens I could not identify. It was most tasty and satisfying." Mandy smiled dreamily as she remembered the delectable concoction.

"But it was no more delicious than the lunch we enjoyed at your fine establishment, sir," added Penelope.

These pleasantries out of the way, a hush fell over the group as they waited for the séance to begin.

The Enchantress gazed around the room with regal slowness, deliberately making prolonged eye contact with each person at the table. This drawnout process made Penelope highly uncomfortable. She never did like people staring her in the eye for more than a second or two. *For Pete's sake, get on with it already!* she wanted to scream, but she kept her carping to herself.

"Beloved friends," the Enchantress finally uttered in a throaty whisper, "let us join hands around this common table, for we assemble on this auspicious occasion to bind our spirits together as one and thus lend the strength of many to our calling forth of spirits from the remote dimension."

Oh, good Lord, thought Penelope. *Do we really have to hold hands like a bunch of kids at a sing—along?* She watched as each person found the hands of their neighbors and grasped them in their own. Mandy's right hand touched Penelope's left hand, and the older woman clasped it readily, for she instinctively trusted her thoughtful young companion. Holding hands with the Enchantress was another matter entirely. Penelope saw the witch's hand being extended toward her graciously, the palm open and turned upward, the slender fingers slightly spread apart, and yet Penelope resisted taking the proffered hand in her own. Why? Was it because she somehow feared or resented the woman, or was it simply that she would feel silly holding hands with a female practically her own age? Her expressive eyes narrowed to mere slits so that she almost appeared to be drowsing, the beautiful and stately witch waited patiently, somehow compelling Penelope to finally give in and take her hand. It was surprisingly warm, the skin smooth and pleasant to the touch. The woman's fingers closed and extended mild pressure on Penelope's hand—just enough to let her know that she was there. *It'll be over with soon,* Penelope assured herself. *Just be patient.* Mandy's left hand was extended into open air, with no one sitting beside her to take hold of it, as was the gypsy's right hand.

After a minute of uncomfortable silence, the Enchantress began to chant in what seemed to be a random combination of archaic English and an obscure foreign tongue. Penelope couldn't make heads or tails of her babbling and quickly stopped trying to understand, preferring instead to gaze around the room, studying the faces of the other guests, each of whom appeared to be lost in their own thoughts.

In the center of the table stood a tall, thin spirit trumpet fashioned of gleaming tin. As the Enchantress chanted mystically, this odd instrument began to tremble and then, suddenly, lifted itself up into the air where it floated above the table top, quivering uncertainly. Penelope assumed this must be a conjurer's trick of some kind, although she saw no wires or other means that could explain the object's levitation. The Enchantress mumbled more loudly and in response a thin, piercing tone issued from the metallic horn. Soon, the damned thing was braying shrilly, like the horn of some demented jazz player condemned to perform in the sordid pits of Hades.

Oh my, thought Penelope. *This is a bit much to take.*

Then Penelope smelled an awful stench that called to mind the sulfurous odor of a match being lit. *Good grief! Has this impostor no shame?*

At this point in the proceedings, the Enchantress pulled out all the stops and launched into what Penelope thought of as full trance mode: twitching, writhing, ranting gutturally, and generally acting up, and with that something really strange began to happen. At each of the three remaining empty chairs placed around the table, a vague luminosity began to form. At first it was nothing more than a faint white glowing zone positioned just above each chair's seat, but after a while these spectral lights began to take on a more full and definite form, and soon Penelope and Mandy were startled to see the ghostly apparitions of three beings condensing out of thin air—human figures who now became seated in the formerly vacant chairs. One of these figures was clearly that of a man materializing next to Mandy, while between him and the gypsy woman, a pair of what was recognizable as female persons began to take shape. The masculine figure extended his ethereal hand and Mandy took it in her own, and then his other hand clasped that of the ghostly woman beside him, and she in turn took the hand of the spectral lady beside her, who then joined hands with the gypsy woman.

Remarkably, Penelope realized that she recognized two of the ghostly visitors. One was certainly the silent film actress, Arkham's own Rebecca Pascal, who had been dead for several years now, and the other was, unbelievably, the great nineteenth-century American author Edgar Allan Poe. She didn't recognize the third specter: a quite proper-looking younger woman. Or maybe she did. Had she seen this refined lady somewhere about town, perhaps at the university? Penelope was searching her memory banks for that distinctive face when she felt a powerful burst of raw energy pulsing through the group like a high–voltage electrical charge conducted from hand to hand, immediately followed by a loud explosion and a brilliant flash of white light, at which instant the five adjacent shapes of Penelope, Mandy, Edgar, Rebecca, and the woman whom Penelope would later learn was named Agnes all disappeared, leaving behind only the empty chairs they had lately occupied.

Chapter XXVII

In the early hours of a crisp autumn morning, the five dimensional travelers found themselves sprawled in random positions of repose in a damp cornfield on an abandoned farm a mile outside of the hag−infested seaport of New Salem, which more than one scholar of eso−terica has claimed is the Dreamland of Witchery's counterpart to the waking−world city of Arkham.

Penelope Armitage was the first of them to come to full con−sciousness. Before she had even opened her eyes to the amber light now bursting through a bank of black clouds on the eastern horizon, she sensed that a great deal of time had passed since the five of them had suddenly disappeared at the séance. It seemed as if days, possibly even weeks had elapsed since that strange midnight session at the mountainside mansion. And it wasn't simply a sense of being dislo−cated in time; the air here felt very different than it had in Dylath−Leen. It was sweeter and richer—as pungent as the exhalations of exotic flowers in a strange garden she might encounter during the delirium that accompanies a grave illness.

Eyes still shut, she recalled the powerful explosion that had im−mediately preceded their transport to this uncanny realm, and with that memory she wondered if she might have been injured by it. But no, apparently she had not been. Her arms and legs were intact and moved as they ought to, and furthermore there was no sensation of pain or stiffness anywhere in her body. In fact, what she was feeling was the deep comfort and satisfaction that came from having slept long and deeply. It was such a pleasant thing that she wished to hold onto it for just a little while longer and considered allowing herself to drift off again into the delicious slumber from which she had just emerged, but that turned out to be impossible, for she had begun to wonder exactly what their situation was here: were they whole and safe, or did this new domain present some element of risk to their freedom and survival? Digging her fingers into the moist loam below her, she slowly raised her eyelids until the surrounding landscape came into focus before her, and then with considerable reluctance she pushed herself up into a slumped position that could pass for sit—ting erect.

"Mandy, dear, are you alive?" she called out softly.

The girl stirred, rubbing her pretty face with hands that were stained a light brown from the bare soil surrounding the pile of yel—lowed husks where she had made her bed.

"I think so. Maybe." Mandy looked around with an expression of unconcealed bewilderment. "Where in heaven's name are we?"

"In a farmer's field . . . corn from the look of it . . . although how we got here I haven't a clue."

"Welcome to the dreamland of witchery, ladies! You can thank me for your passage, which required more than a casual knowledge of magick on my part, I can assure you!" said a wily feminine voice that, to Penelope's mind, oozed a kind of hardened confidence that was tainted by strains of arrogance.

Penelope and Mandy simultaneously turned their heads and saw that the speaker was a stunningly beautiful woman in a shimmering gown reclining gracefully in the field a short distance behind them, her voluptuous figure propped up on one elbow. Both recognized the woman from the many photographs of her they had seen over the years, and particularly recently as they worked with her archive at the university library. Although it was clearly in violation of the laws of nature, the woman was none other than the late film star Rebecca Pascal.

"Pardon my saying so, but you're not supposed to be here," stated Penelope flatly. "You're quite dead, madame."

Rebecca threw back her head and laughed riotously. "And yet, *voilà,* here I am! Ha ha ha! That's but one of the countless wonders of this marvelous place, my darlings. Yes, I am as 'dead as a door–knob,' as we used to say back in my misspent youth, and even worse, my very soul was cruelly devoured by that traitorous bastard Ka–mog—I'm sure you heard about that; it was the talk of the town. However, there remained a small portion of my soul, my 'essence,' if you will, that Kamog could not touch and it lived on in the lands of dream, where I had cleverly hidden it from him. That itty–bitty piece of my indomitable spirit did not die, nor shall it ever!" Look–ing up to the sky as if to make a direct address to the malign entity from Outside, she shook her fist and screamed mockingly, "Eat your heart out, Kamog!"

At this point a male voice broke the spell that Rebecca was cast–ing over the two women. "Prithee, my lady, might you please keep it down? Your caterwauling is making my head throb something awful," pleaded Poe, standing upright with a visible degree of effort so that he might more effectively brush the dirt and leaves from his crumpled black suit.

"Oh, settle down, Edgar," replied Rebecca dismissively. "It's time you were up and about anyway. Daylight's burning, and we have places to go and people to see."

"This early?"

"Yes, we have urgent business to attend to. Our destinies await us, Mr. Poe."

"If we must . . ." He examined his nails as if he suspected they were secret enemies.

With all the commotion going on about her, Agnes Aspinwall began to stir. Lifting one puffy eye from where it had been pressed against a flat clod, she inquired in a trembling voice, "Have we hot tea, Ms. Pascal? I'm not a morning person at all, and I really must have tea if you people insist on continuing to shout at one another at this ungodly hour."

"All right, get up, all of you," Rebecca commanded, weary of the grousing. "Rise and shine! I have a hunch we'll find all the pro–visions we need at the farmhouse. If I recall, a demented old crone lives there as a squatter. No doubt she'll have food and drink a—plenty, if we can convince her we're genuine folk of the Craft and not the spectral manifestations of the terrible Dark Man who alleg—edly haunts the local woods."

The lot of them now up and awake, they drifted toward the squat, ramshackle farmhouse where a faint yellow light glimmered in one window—a sure sign that the crone was indeed at home.

★

Unnoticed by the five companions, one other figure had magi—cally materialized in the cornfield that morning. This sixth person was Mandy's would—be suitor, the sandy—haired member of the Smoke and Ash Society named Charles Morelle—or, as Mandy liked to refer to him, the 'creepy graduate student.' He had been sprawled out on tilled soil a short distance from the group; but, being on the other side of a small mound of cornstalks, he had been out of the line of sight of the others. Coming to consciousness shortly after Penelo—pe had, and soon after he heard voices nearby, he had kept himself very still and quiet so as not to give away his presence. It was only after the group had gotten up and began walking toward the farm—house that he arose, brushed himself off, and stealthily followed them from a safe distance so as not to be detected.

His arrival in the dreamland of witchery was something of an accident, if not a miracle. As was his custom, he had been sitting in the Hobo Bean Coffee Company, sipping a French Roast brew and staring lasciviously at the poster for the Mexican film *Demonio del Sol,* while repeating over and over again in his mind the words from a powerful magick ritual that he had heard the night before at a meeting of the Society, when suddenly his surroundings began to fade away and in their place a strange scene came into view. Instead of sitting at a table in a well—lit coffee shop in Arkham, he was now sitting on a bench in a dark trolley that was parked at the base of a mountain on the edges of the town of Dylath—Leen. The conductor and motorman, who had been doing their maintenance chores be—fore locking up the station for the night, immediately seized him and demanded that he state his business. Terrified what these two bizarre beings might do to him, Charles had confessed all: his foolish dabbling in magick, his stalking of Mandy, his desire to contact the supernatural entity Kamog just as Rebecca Pascal had once notoriously done. Hearing all this, the two men—if that's what they were—laughed heartily.

"We can't help you any with luring down that Kamog fellow," said the conductor, poking Charles in the ribs with an elbow, "but we'll give you a hand at getting together with your sweetheart, Miss Mandy." When they went up to the mansion later that evening to perform their duties related to the séance, they brought Charles along with them, first sneaking him into the Master's house and then into the upstairs room where the ritual was to be performed. A heavy velvet curtain hung across the back wall behind the table where the séance would take place. They instructed him to hide himself behind that curtain until the guests had arrived and the séance had begun. During her incantations, they explained, the Enchantress would say a certain phrase which they gave him. At that moment, they told him, if he reached out his hand through the slit in the curtains and placed it gently on the shoulder of a young woman named Agnes who would be seated nearest to where he was standing, he would become part of the circle of practitioners who were spiritually bonded together by the holding of hands. The same energy that flowed through them would flow through him, and when the members of Mandy's party were transported to the dreamland of witchery, Charles would be among them. Charles couldn't believe his luck: not only would he be with Mandy, but he would gain entrance into the legendary dreamland of witchery. It was almost too good to be true.

"But won't this Agnes woman feel my hand on her shoulder and cry out in alarm, exposing me?"

"Not with all that energy coursing through her body, she won't. She won't even notice it, and then *bang!*—you'll all find yourselves in another realm, wherever the magick takes you."

Chapter XXVIII

Agnes watched as a raven flew over the cornfield and landed on the chimney of the old farmhouse. The fowl seemed a larger specimen of its species than she had ever encountered in the waking world, and it was a bit unnerving the way the bird seemed to observe their movement to the ancient residence of the crone. Agnes prepared to knock timidly on the door, but Rebecca swept past her and pushed the door open, not hesitating to stride into the main living chamber, a spacious room with an extraordinarily high ceiling. Near that ceiling, balanced on a carpet composed of straw and features, floated the mistress of the place, holding an elaborate brush with which she painted sigils onto the smooth plaster with which the ceiling was composed.

"Hoo—hoo, we have company!" the woman hooted, as the large raven darted into the room from one of its small windows and perched on the crone's shoulder. The visitors stood patiently as the crone rustled the large sleeves of her yellow gown—sleeves that, in their movement, resembled the wings of a monstrous mutant butterfly; and then the carpet sank to the floor of antique wooden planks, and the crone waved her hands to the group in greeting. "There is a table in that corner there, with food and drink a—plenty. Abide, if ye feel the need for sustenance."

Edgar approached the woman and knelt before her, holding to her his hand. "We thank you for your hospitality, madam. I find myself especially thirsty."

"There is a bottle of dreamland brandy especially for you, poet. Nay, do not look astounded. I beheld your arrival in my glass ball. What an odd assembly you are, the lot of you. This dreamland of witchery has never seen such a perverse crew of dwellers. You are like a bundle of rare herbs bound together for the spicing of some outrageous brew, each with its distinct flavor and effect. How delicious it is to drink such concoction, as I sup on your combined effect within this realm." She squinted her eyes. "And yet, you are incomplete—for there is another who has followed you, one who is unwelcome and linked in some subtle way to the manifestations of Nyarlathotep, that defiler of mortal dreaming." With effort, the elder creature stood and hobbled to a table. "But enough prattle, come and feast. And if you have no fear, let me ladle a measure of rare potion from that steaming cauldron into your cups, the taste of which will help to fortify ye for the wonders you may yet encounter."

"We thank you," Rebecca answered as she led her group to the table.

The crone studied the film actress for some few seconds and then bent to Rebecca and whispered. "You come like some flickering specter into this realm, and you corrupt the air with wickedness. They cannot see you as the monster that ye are, lucky sods. You would be wise to contain your deviltry while here—for wickedness can attract its likeness in ways that even you could not control."

Edgar stood some little ways from the rest of the group, a bottle of brandy in one hand and a half-empty cognac glass in the other. Bringing the glass to his nostrils, he imagined that he could smell a remnant of the oak casks in which the liquor had been aged. The illumination from a nearby candle danced within the gold-tinted glass and the fluid it contained; and as Edgar peered into the ambiance inside the glass he held, he began to fancy fantastic things. Gazing into one corner of the room, he imagined that he saw a large raven peering at him, and that one of the creature's large eyes was grotesquely blemished. Quickly, the poet gulped the rest of the liquor in his glass.

"Are ye all on foot? Such a slow way to wander, and the dream-land of witchery is wide. Alas, I have but one broom, for 'tis a won-drous thing to ride our brooms on the wind through moonlit mist!"

Agnes plopped a juicy grape into her mouth, and then used a ti-ny knife to slice off a portion of smooth cheese. Food had never tasted more delicious, and she couldn't understand if that was the ef-fect of eating in a dreamland realm or if the quality of this repast was of a higher order than that found in the waking world. She couldn't stop shoveling in mouthfuls of food, and yet she didn't begin to feel heavy, bloated, or full. But the crone shuffled to her and placed a restraining hand upon her own.

"You need to slow down, dear, or daemon-slumber will over-take ye. It is not wise to sleep while in this realm, for then one is tempted to dream within a dream, and such reverie can be daemon-ic. Ah, just as I thought, your forehead grows hot and your eyes heavy." Raising the hand that was not pressed against the younger woman's face, the crone's fingers moved in an esoteric way to the raven, and the others watched as the bulky bird spread its wings and drifted so as to settle on the crone's outstretched arm. Bending her face to the raven's head, the antique woman began to whisper a mysterious song, and then she bent her head back and the bird's great wings began to flap ferociously so that an enchanted movement of air sailed to Agnes's face. Edgar walked a little nearer to Agnes and watched as tiny particles of darkness fell from the girl's eyes, until those eyes grew bright and alert. The poet then raised his bottle of brandy to the glass he held, poured a small amount of liqueur into the glass, and offered it to Agnes.

The crone nodded as she watched. "Come, then, my company of friends, and I will help aid thee on thy way."

Chapter XXIX

Hobbling along the deeply rutted path that meandered from the aged farmhouse to the sagging barn with the aid of a gnarled walking stick, the old crone was followed by the party of four witches and one poet. Trailing furtively behind them at a safe distance was the graduate student, Charles Morelle, who concealed his presence behind various bushes and farm implements he encountered along the way until the witches and Poe had entered the barn. Then he made so bold as to openly approach the barn without benefit of cover, positioning himself where he could peer into the building through a crack between the large wooden door that had been swung open wide by the crone and the frame upon which it hung.

"I love barns!" Mandy exclaimed, running up to a pile of hay and falling into it with her arms and legs spread−eagled.

"Dearie," the crone corrected, "properly speaking, this be a stable, not a barn, but you can call it that if you fancy." As if on cue, a pony in one of the shadowy stalls whinnied. "You'll need sturdy mounts, five of 'em. This little moke won't bear the likes of any of you with the possible exception of Mandy here, although she'd do for a shriveled−up ol' hag like me. Nar, we need five good steeds to carry you folks to your destination point . . ."

"Which is where, exactly?" interrupted Penelope.

"All in good time, dearie, all in good time. There's no sense in getting too far ahead of yerselves. As I was saying, five good steeds . . ." The crone looked around the stable, eyeing the stacks of rusty tools, outdated supplies, and busted—up junk that were stashed in every nook and cranny of the dilapidated structure.

"Aha! There's what we need!"

From atop a teetering pile of antique torture devices abandoned in a cobweb—draped corner, the crone plucked an odd device that vaguely resembled a helmet except that it consisted of narrow metal straps crisscrossing the wearer's skull that would offer little protection against the depredations of a sword or battle axe.

"A witch's bridle!" The crone hugged the strange instrument to her bosom.

"Pray tell," said Penelope. "I haven't seen one of those in years."

"What is it?" asked Mandy, eyes wide with wonder.

Penelope explained. "In the days of persecution, these things were put over women's heads to shut them up or humble them. And not just in the case of a woman being accused of witchcraft. They were also used against any woman who spoke out of turn, or nagged men, or otherwise annoyed the elite members of the community, who always happened to be men. It's strapped to the victim's head with an iron bit that goes inside her mouth. The bit has sharp prongs on it that dig into her tongue and cheeks if the lady attempts to speak her mind. Vile instruments of torment and abuse, if you ask me."

"Indeed they are," agreed the crone, "but they have another use, I've found—one less well—known. Watch and learn, dearies."

The old woman quickly fashioned five piles of straw in each of five empty horse stalls. Then, one by one, she lay the witch's bridle upon the pile for a few seconds, and each mound of straw turned in—to a living, snorting, black stallion as she mouthed the oath "Whisk!"

"Whisk . . . whisk . . . whisk . . . whisk!"

"Bravo!" proclaimed the moderately inebriated Edgar, raising his brandy bottle.

Mandy clapped enthusiastically while Agnes and Penelope issued appreciative "oohs" and "aahs."

"Well done indeed, madame!" Rebecca granted, placing a friendly hand on the crone's shoulder.

"I learnt summat in my hundred years, I did! You'll find saddles, blankets, bridles—the regular leather kind, I mean—stirrups, and other riding gear scattered about. Help yourselves to whatever you need!"

From his hiding place behind the door, the frustrated Charles watched helplessly as the party of five gleefully mounted their horses and rode away from the stable amid a thunderous roar of pounding hooves, leaving him behind to deal with the crone's wrath, should she discover him.

The crone nodded to her familiar perched high above in the rafters, the raven studying her with its one good eye. Knowing her intent, the huge black bird took to the air and made a beeline for the departing riders.

"Foller the corbie," she screeched out to the riders. "He knows the way!"

Poe, who was on the last horse in the pack, looked back at her with a tipsy smile and waved wildly to show that he had heard, almost falling out of his saddle in the process.

"Goddess help 'em," muttered the crone to no one in particular, although she realized that Charles stood nearby and heard her every word. "Where they're going, they'll need it, poor buggers. Now as for ye, good sir," she said, swinging the door shut on its squeaky hinges and exposing the terrified grad student, "whatever are I to do with ye?"

CHAPTER XXX

Charles Morelle squirmed uncomfortably under the hostile gaze of the century–old crone. Physically, of course, he knew he could take her. She was tiny, frail, and arthritic; he could easily pick her up bodily, throw her in the stable, and bolt the door. However, she had one huge advantage over the sandy–haired graduate student: her advanced skill in the magickal arts, gained over the course of a lifetime of practice.

"Aha! I detect a dark design forming in yer bony head, young man! Just try laying hands on a seasoned adept and ye'll live to regret it—should I chose to spare yer life!"

"You're right, old woman, I can't hope to overpower you by brute force alone. That would indeed be foolish to even attempt. But you don't hold all the cards, crone. I've got a trick or two up my sleeve."

"Have ye now? Just try it."

He wasn't bluffing. There was one powerful piece of magick at his disposal that she knew nothing about. It was the second, so far unused, part of the spoken ritual that had gotten him to dreamland in the first place. The fellows in the Smoke and Ash Society called it "the callback." The first phrase in the two–part ritual would—they claimed—help transport his spirit to the dreamlands, while leaving his physical body unoccupied and dormant in the waking world. And it had worked. He had mentally spoken the first phrase while meditating in a coffee shop in Arkham, and a moment later had found himself sitting in an idle trolley on the fringes of Dylath–Leen.

What the callback phrase was primarily designed to do was to allow the user's soul to return to his unoccupied body at some point in the future after his business in the dreamlands was completed. And that's how he had originally intended to use it.

But there was a little–known variant use to which the callback phrase could be put in a pinch. If it was uttered while staring hyp–notically into the eyes of some hapless adversary in any of the many dreamlands, that person's soul would be instantly transported back to the user's physical body in the waking world, and would go on to oc–cupy it indefinitely as if it were the person's own body, while the speaker of the ritual would take her place in her now unoccupied as–tral body in the dreamlands. In effect, Charles had the power to trade bodies with the crone. He could force her into his material body in the waking world—the body of a young male in good health—while he took over her non–material body in the dreamland of witchery—the decrepit frame of an elderly beldame. There was nothing she could do to prevent this, and she wouldn't even see it coming.

"Why stare ye so hard, boy, and what claptrap do ye mumble? Yer evil eye has no sway upon me!"

Those were the last words she spoke before her spirit fled the scene and Charles found himself looking out through her aged, cata–ract–fogged eyes. His own astral body was nowhere to be seen, for it had been purely a manifestation of his soul before he took control of the crone's astral body.

Taking the crone's cane from where she had left it leaning against the side of the stable, Charles hobbled over to the little pony in the far stall and, with considerable effort, climbed upon its back and rode away in the same direction in which Rebecca Pascal and her companions had departed moments ago.

Meanwhile, in Arkham, once she got beyond the initial shock of finding herself trapped in Charles Morelle's body, the crone was be–side herself with joy. Not only was it delightful to be young again, but she'd always secretly wanted to be a man instead of a woman. So much more was possible in this world when you were male, or so she'd heard. Oh, the wicked things she would do!

Chapter XXXI

Penelope, having trouble balancing on her saddle as the horses moved through dreamland, squinted at Rebecca, whose animal was in the lead. "You needn't rush ahead of us as if you were the leader of the pack," Penelope grumbled.

Without looking behind her, Rebecca replied, "Someone has to assume a role of authority—and it isn't likely to be someone as ridiculous and flighty as you, my dear."

Edgar, a bit bleary-eyed, raised his head a little and tried to appear imperial. "As the male among us, I—"

"Can it, Poe!" Penelope instantly interrupted. She shook her head derisively. "Really, you're both nothing but manifestations of dream or spirit or some such ridiculous thing. *I'm still living!* When this is all over, I return to reality, while you two will fade into shadow and memory." She paused in her speech to admire its poetry. Perhaps associating with these two was having an aesthetic effect that enhanced her feeling for poetic language. She would explore this when she returned to the land of wakefulness. Suddenly, she was distracted by a small shadow that passed over them, and she turned to frown at Edgar as he laughed softly to himself.

"My winged friend serves as our Divine Herald. Lead on, grim and ancient guide!" He then noticed that Rebecca had brought her horse to a halt, and when he followed her example he saw that she seemed to be listening intently to some subdued sound.

"Now that's ridiculous—smog in a dream world," Penelope complained as she pointed ahead of them. They all looked at the wall

149

of haze toward which the raven swooped, and Agnes couldn't comprehend what was *wrong* with that wall, why it seemed to shift and waver, like a living entity. Edgar shouted in alarm as his feathery friend sailed through that wall as if it were but an apparition and no solid thing.

Rebecca held up a hand so as to silence the others. "Listen," she advised them. At first they could detect no sound; and then, slowly, it came to them, from the distant wall—a sound of eldritch windsong, very faint and utterly alien. "Can you hear it—its awful articulation? It calls us forth." She shook her horse's reins and shouted a few words, and the others reluctantly followed her as Rebecca moved toward the wavering miasmic wall.

"Do you know what it reminds me of?" asked Agnes. "Isn't there a legend that the original name of the *Necronomicon*—*Al Azif*—signifies the howling of a desert wind that sounds like the buzzing of a million insects? I've often wondered what that could possibly resemble—and here it is." Her eyes were shimmering with wonder as she listened, and she did begin to catch the 'articulation' mentioned by Rebecca—the eerie semblance of pronounced language that might have been spoken by some unearthly thing. Agnes then shouted in shock and dismay as, unexpectedly, Rebecca geed her horse and sped toward the wall, and then passed through it, as if into some alternative dimension.

Edgar turned to look at Agnes, and he smiled mischievously. "Come, my lady, let us pass through the veil!" He kicked at his horse, and the animal carried him through the buzzing barrier. Moving off her saddle, Agnes floated to the ground, and like some tender mother she guided her beast toward the humming wall of haze. As she drew near to it she realized that it was in fact a curtain of living things, millions upon millions of colorful winged insects. She passed slowly through them, not blinking as she knew the trembling of their wings upon her eyes. Those eyes drank in the shimmering whiteness of the scene before her, of the pearl-like sand that was a desert floor, and the bleached pillars that towered above that sand, pillars on which secret symbols had been etched. Above her

stretched a colorless sky, and in that sky she beheld a smooth revolv-
ing orb that was not sun or moon. Edgar's horse had stopped beside
one hoary pillar, and the poet was leaning so as to study the symbols,
over which he smoothed his small hand.

"You look pensive," Agnes informed the poet.

Edgar nodded. "It's perplexing—and intriguing. I have no rec-
ollection of ever viewing such sigils as these; and yet, looking on
them now, I can read and pronounce their rare language."

Although he felt a tinge of caution, the poet began to chant; and
as the language escaped his lips, the pale disc above them, which was
neither moon nor sun, began to blacken. Everyone raised their eyes
and watched the silhouette of the raven as it floated before the image
of the orb; and then Agnes gasped as that fowl began to fluctuate and
flow in form as it expanded impossibly. The transformed bird, now
gigantic, drifted to where Edgar stood and cocked its head as if it
would convey some message to the writer. Nodding, the poet
climbed onto the bird's massive back and took hold of feathers with
both hands. "Spread your condor wings, fine fellow, and show me
the secret places in this world of dream!" Gracefully, the feathered
behemoth lifted itself and Poe from earth, toward the shadows in the
sky; and when they vanished into those shadows the others could
hear Edgar's dimming cry of *"Tekeli-li! Tekeli-li!"*

Chapter XXXII

Agnes watched the dark form that vanished within the shadows in the sky, from which a mortal cry still echoed; and then a gentle wind floated to her from the clouds in that sky, and carried on the air‒stream was a fragrance such as she had never inhaled. The wind was warm when it first touched her face; but as it passed her she sensed the air grew colder, and its humming became a low moaning, sounding like some doomed soul who bewailed existence. The ter‒rain of this section of dreamland blurred before her and grew pale, and when she slipped off her beast and stood, her feet sank into a field of shifting sand. Rebecca, standing suddenly beside her, took the younger woman's hand and guided her across the sand, past the shapeless foundations of half‒buried houses and shrines, until they came to the hoary remnant of a temple of unwholesome antiquity.

"We cannot open the portal on our own," the elder witch in‒formed Agnes, "for we wear too much of human taint. Let me summon a keeper who can assist us."

Reaching into a pocket, Rebecca produced a small satin bag, its opening tied shut with a slender length of golden string. She untied the string and shook the cloth bag over the place where she stood, and Agnes watched the black and gold sand that spilled from the bag and mingled with the surface on which they stood. Agnes watched as a portion of the mingled sand began to churn and rise as a petite whirlwind, and Rebecca chortled as the roiling particles wove to‒gether so as to form a fantastic figure that refused to solidify with completion. Agnes thought that the wavering creature almost re‒

sembled Sobek, a deity of ancient Egypt; and when the beast parted
the elongated snout that served as mouth, a diseased buzzing filtered
into the air as ghostly articulation.

Agnes listened as Rebecca engaged in dialogue with the specter
of sand, and then she could not repress a gasp as that bestial phantom
glided to the great iron doors of the temple and passed through them
as if they were composed of liquid. The doors began to break apart,
and then their substance drifted to the ground and formed twin
mounds of debris that were blown apart and strewn about by the
cold howling wind.

★

Mandy and Penelope were so transfixed by the vision of Mr. Poe
grandly flying off on the back of the enlarged raven and dramatically
disappearing into a shadowy patch of sky that they failed to observe
that Rebecca and Agnes had pierced the living wall of humming insects ahead of them and entered a mysterious desert city.

"Oh, dear," said Penelope, finally coming to her senses. "We've
been left behind. Let's not dawdle, Mandy. I don't relish being on
our own in this strange environment."

"It's okay, they're just ahead. I can see their shapes through the
clouds of flying bugs."

As had Rebecca and Agnes before them, Penelope and Mandy
effortlessly penetrated the shimmering wall, their horses shuffling
slowly through the millions of swarming insects.

"It tickles!" said Mandy, laughing softly as the insects brushed
their wings against her face.

"Better than stinging," replied Penelope in her usual cynical tone.

"True. That would be a serious problem, there are so many of
them!"

"We would need a veritable ocean of lotion, as the old song goes."

"What song is that, Penelope?"

"Never mind, dear—it's from way before your time."

Once they had cleared the curtain of tiny buzzing creatures, the
two women dismounted and entered the ancient city on foot, leav-

ing their horses behind to forage among the rubble of broken stones for some vegetation to graze upon.

"Do you still see them, dear?" asked Penelope with mounting concern that they could be left behind by the faster-moving Rebecca and Agnes. As witches of some experience, those two knew how to get along in a place like this, while she and Mandy were clearly out of their league.

"Not exactly, but I believe they entered that temple over there—the big building almost buried in the sand. That's the direction they were headed when I last could make out their silhouettes."

"Then that's where we need to go, and quickly."

★

Rebecca led the way, authoritatively striding into the ancient temple through the portal that had just been opened by the crocodile-snouted simulacrum as if she owned the place.

"Come along, dear. We haven't all day."

"Are you sure it's safe?" asked Agnes. "What about snakes or spiders? What if there are rats?"

"Then we'll deal with them. No vermin is a match for me, I assure you."

"Okay . . . if you think it's safe."

"Nothing in life is safe. You should know better than that."

The younger witch hesitantly followed Rebecca into a small atrium area just beyond the entrance where the heavy iron doors had lately hung. It was fairly well lit from the rays of daylight that fell through the entryway—well enough for the women to see that three separate rooms opened off of this small preliminary chamber. One passageway lay straight ahead, while the other two were on the left and right sides.

Against the wall near the main entrance lay a pile of rough sticks of various sizes that Rebecca recognized were meant to be used as torches. Each had been coated in some flammable material—probably pitch, judging from its black, gooey consistency. She picked up two and handed one of them to Agnes.

"These will light our journey through the building."

Agnes fumbled eagerly in her pocket. "I might have matches," she explained. "Not that I'm a smoker, but for candles and incense."

"No need for that. Don't forget we are in the dreamland of witchery and my powers—and yours—are much keener here than in the waking world or even the dreamland of men." Rebecca thrust her torch out in front of her, tightly gripping it at the base with one hand, while she waved the palm of her other hand over its coated end. The head of the torch burst into bright yellow flame. *"Voilà!"*

"Well done, Rebecca!"

The older witch touched the head of Agnes's torch with her own, lighting it, and then walked toward the middle passageway, the better to inspect the inscription carved in the stone above.

Agnes tarried for a moment, not immediately joining Rebecca. She grabbed a pair of the other torches, jammed their handles into the sand covering the floor along the base of the wall, and lit the up-right sticks with her own torch.

"I'm leaving a couple of these lit for Penelope and Mandy, so they'll be able to follow us when they do catch up."

"Why bother with that, my dear? To hell with them. They are both so boringly mundane, and that Armitage woman is absurdly dreary. Let them fend for themselves, if they can."

Agnes said nothing in response, not wanting to annoy Rebecca and raise her ire, but nonetheless she left the torches burning for their tardy companions.

"It looks to be some infernal script from antediluvian times," said Rebecca, squinting at the exotic figures cut into the wall above the middle doorway. "I can't make heads or tails of it."

"Allow me to attempt a translation," said Agnes. "An uncle of mine was an Egyptologist, and when he visited us in the summers when I was a girl he would teach me some of the rudimentary hieroglyphics that were commonly used in the Nile valley during antiquity. I'm certainly no expert, but I might be able to pick out a word or two."

"I'm impressed. Be my guest." Rebecca stood aside as Agnes

approached closer and stared at the inscription, raising her torch high so that the flames almost licked at the carved figures.

"Um . . . I think that symbol, the third one on the left, is 'Tar'—it means 'path' or 'way,' and the one at the far right means 'Vanity.' The symbol to its left that looks like a comb with its teeth facing up means 'Men,' I think. If all that's true, then possibly this door is the 'Path of the Men of Vanity,' or less literally, 'Path of Vain Men.'"

From where they stood they could see that this middle door opened onto a narrow passageway with a low ceiling about five feet tall, which would require them to bow down if they decided to follow it. The tunnel−like passageway burrowed deep into the structure for at least a hundred feet, beyond which lay impenetrable darkness.

"Oh, that doesn't sound very promising. We'd best not go that way. How about this one over here?" asked Rebecca, turning to her left. She held her torch up to the inscription above the second door, which they could see opened into a much roomier space with high ceilings.

Agnes studied it for almost a minute, before announcing "It's almost the same as the first inscription, except that where the first one had the symbol for 'Vanity' this one has the symbol for 'Upright.'"

"Making it the 'Path of Upright Men'?"

"Quite possibly, although I don't know if it means 'upright' as in 'upstanding,' or literally 'erect,' as in standing upright, i.e., *Homo erectus*. At any rate, that sounds far more welcoming in my opinion, even if we aren't technically men."

"Gender probably doesn't factor into it, I suppose."

"Likely not."

A pair of alabaster statutes of muscular men with noble faces flanked the doorway on the left.

"And this last one on the right?" asked Rebecca.

Agnes walked up to it and stared long and hard before speaking. "Again, it's nearly the same as the other two inscriptions, but I'm having trouble with the one variable symbol. I want to say it's 'low' or 'flat,' but that doesn't make much sense, does it?"

"Maybe it does. Look at the ceiling in there—it's only two or three feet tall. Not very accommodating to upright men. And those carved figures lining the walls: they look like crocodiles. What if the symbol means 'Prostrate'? Could it be the 'Path of Prostrate Men'?"

"Oh, you might be right! Maybe it's the 'Path of Prostrate Men.' But what sort of men crawl on their bellies, face down? How nasty. Might they be some reptilian deities worshipped by the ancients who built this temple, which were in the shape of men but with heads like crocodiles?"

"Yes. That explains why an image resembling the ancient deity Sobek miraculously appeared to open the portal for us. Good job, Agnes! You are a useful little wench after all! We'll take the doorway on the left. I'm not getting down on my belly to crawl into some stinking hole built for alligators, that's for damned sure! We'll go the other way, the 'Way of the Upright Men.'"

Agnes agreed that was the wisest choice.

Chapter XXXIII

Entering the passageway which Agnes had tentatively identified as representing the "Path of Upright Men" according to its ancient builders, the two women found themselves in a spacious chamber whose walls were so remote that they were just barely visible in the feeble light emitted by the torches. Evenly distributed throughout the vast room were stout pillars of carved stone that served to support the chamber's ornate ceiling of engraved marble slabs.

"What purpose could this big empty room have possibly served?" asked Agnes, not really expecting an answer.

"Perhaps crowds assembled here during some sort of ceremony or ritual," speculated Rebecca.

"Yes, I can picture that."

"Let's go have a closer look at that far wall, the one straight ahead. Maybe that will tell us more."

Rebecca strode off in a tremendous hurry, as if she had an urgent appointment across the room and dare not be late. Agnes was forced to walk at a faster than comfortable pace to keep up with the older witch. As they crossed the wide expanse of floor it soon became apparent that there was a break of some sort in the pattern of white pavement stones ahead—a darker, circular area of about fifty feet in diameter. Once they were within a hundred feet of this anomaly, it became obvious that what they were seeing was actually a huge hole in the floor, a cylindrical shaft that burrowed down into the lower levels of what must have been a gigantic architectural structure.

"Well, now," Rebecca called back over her shoulder to Agnes, who was struggling to keep up. "This is starting to get interesting!"

"Whatever is the hurry, Rebecca?"

"No hurry, my dear, but why dilly–dally? Have you better things to do right now?"

"Yes, I suppose you're correct. I could use a cup of tea, however–er."

"I'm afraid there's going to be no tea in our afternoon, Agnes. Best forget such amenities. But if we can find that which we seek and get back to civilization before darkness falls, we just may be able to have ourselves a dinner tonight."

"Oh, dear. That doesn't sound very promising . . ."

They reached the edge of the large opening and peered over its side. What they saw below them lining the walls of the shaft was a spiral stone stairway that began on the level of the chamber they were in and twisted endlessly downward in a clockwise manner, with a small landing at each of the floors below, and the bottom of the shaft lost in darkness.

"Oh, my," said Agnes. "This is a bit ominous."

"It needn't be. I find it rather tantalizing, actually. Just think of it: the forbidden lure of eldritch subterranean mysteries, the almost erotic attraction of ineffable pits of interminable blackness. Come, let's explore its depths!"

"Must we?"

"Yes, we must. Nothing ventured, nothing gained."

Rebecca took the lead, gracefully gliding down the ancient stone steps with Agnes close at her heels, the details of each portion of the shaft's walls coming alive in the sweeping light of their torches as they passed by and then returning to a state of darkness as they con–tinued their descent. One time Rebecca looked back at the younger witch, smiling wildly, and Agnes observed that her eyes had taken on a manic energy that made them shine in the dark like those of a cat. In fact, she looked positively possessed—or at least much more en–thused than Agnes had ever seen her during their sojourn through the dreamlands. For a woman who, at the time of her earthly pass–

ing, was of an advanced age, she was still uncommonly beautiful. Agnes wished she had half of Rebecca's vitality, let alone the older woman's consummate skills in the craft they shared.

At each level Rebecca paused for a moment to scan the gloomy side chambers extending off of the landings, as if she somehow knew that some valuable thing was to be found on one of the many floors below them, if only she were able to read the subtle signs of its presence. At selected landings she lingered longer than at others, but always in the end she dismissed each side chamber as not being the one they sought.

"What are you looking for?" asked Agnes, not sure that Rebecca would hear her now that the older witch was a full floor below her and descending even more rapidly than she had for the first twenty levels.

"Why, of course, I'm looking for the one thing that brought us here to the dreamland of witchery, besides my sincere desire to help you establish yourself as a proper witch in this perfect environment for young, developing crones. We seek the Key of Shadow! Not being allowed to fetch it herself, that nasty Edith Gnome has sent you here on an errand to find it for her, and my role—beyond acting as your tutor and protector—is to help you accomplish that task, dubious as it may be."

"But this is not where the Key of Darkness and Death resides, is it? I thought it was traditionally believed that the Key of Blackness, which unlocks the secrets of the Worm and opens the realms between death and dream, lies hidden in the caverns of the twin-peaked Mount K'nath. Surely we are nowhere near that stone edifice, are we?"

Still racing down slimy steps into darkness, Rebecca breathlessly called out in reply, "Geographically, no, we aren't. But geography isn't an absolute law of the Cosmos. Metaphysically, we are very close to the recesses of K'nath. The wall of invisible energy that separates these sunken desert hollows from the elevated caves of K'nath is but a shimmering phantom in the forgotten dream of a slumbering night-gaunt. Penetrate that gossamer boundary and the

Key is ours!—or Edith's, if you decide to turn it over to her. Personally, if I were you, I'd keep it, but I always have been a selfish bitch."

"A 'shimmering phantom' in a night-gaunt's dream is somehow the same as a vast stretch of land between a desert and a mountain? I'm afraid I really don't understand, Rebecca, but if you say so, I'll take your word for it," answered Agnes in tones so soft she suspected Rebecca may not have heard.

Thus it went for what seemed like hours to Agnes: Rebecca frantically racing down the endlessly spiraling stairs, glancing hurriedly into a tenebrous chamber at each landing before dashing ever downward, with Agnes doing her best to keep up even though she fell further and further behind the deeper they descended. The side chambers, from what little Agnes could see as she quickly passed by each one and her torch illuminated their recesses for a fleeting second, were a chaotic combination of storeroom, shrine, and catacomb. Massive quantities of goods had been deposited in them untold centuries ago. In addition to the rooms' more mundane contents, a number of them held what appeared to be religious altars and relics, and many were packed with thousands upon thousands of neatly piled human bones. How Rebecca would ever find anything as small as a key in such a vast array of junk crammed into so many hundreds of chambers was beyond Agnes's comprehension, but that didn't seem to be a concern for the older witch. Some sort of mad vision drove her tirelessly onward until finally, when Agnes thought she would drop from exhaustion, Rebecca stopped dead at one particular landing that seemed to Agnes to be no different from the others.

"Here, this is the one. The Key is in here." Rebecca slowly entered the chamber, her gown sweeping the floor behind her. By the time Agnes reached the same landing, Rebecca was already deep within the dank, eerie space, studying the ancient carvings incised upon a span of granite wall opposite the doorway. "Yes, this is where the Key is kept. Just beyond this wall. Look here, Agnes: the wall is solid except for this small hole in the center. The key is in a sealed space behind that wall, and the hole is not big enough for a child's hand to pass through."

"How will we get it? Is there some secret door in the wall?"

"There is no hidden door nor sliding panel, just this tiny hole. Its diameter can't be more than two inches. But a snake could slither through there quite easily, wouldn't you say? And look here; we just happen to have a nice little snake on hand who would be more than willing to fetch the Key for us!" Rebecca bent over and picked up off the floor a brass figurine in the shape of a snake that was about a foot in length and an inch in diameter. It was one of several random items littering the floor that apparently had been discarded as worth— less by tomb robbers in bygone ages.

Cooing as she stroked the brass snake with her long tapered fin— gers, Rebecca's eyes flared dramatically until a rich golden light shone from out of her eye sockets and onto the inanimate figurine, making it glow brightly as if the metal had become molten. Magi— cally, the brass snake came to life in her hands and began to coil and squirm. She held it up to the hole in the stone, forcing its head into the black aperture until the reptile relented and bent to her will, crawling into the hole and disappearing into the space behind the wall. A few seconds later, the creature reemerged, a fabulous key of gleaming black metal tightly grasped in its jaws. The beast slithered into Rebecca's hands and obligingly dropped the key into her open palm. Then, as suddenly as it had come to life, it returned to its for— mer inanimate state as a simple brass figurine. Rebecca let the brass snake fall from her hands to the floor where it clanged loudly, send— ing echoes through the recesses of the shadowy chamber. She sud— denly thrust the black object upward, almost poking Agnes in the nose with it, and proclaimed triumphantly, "I present to you the Key of Shadows!"

Chapter XXXIV

Penelope, increasingly confused by the events experienced in the dreamland, chattered (mostly to herself) as her eyes darted about at the incredible place in which she found herself; and then she began to shriek as she noticed Mandy on her hands and knees, crawling through the opening into the shrine. Ignoring the shrill noise, Mandy crept into the chamber called "The Path of Prostrate Men," and as she made her way the chamber's ceiling became lower until only a child, or perhaps some half−human hybrid, could stand erect within the space. But Mandy found that she didn't want to stand, for the texture of the floor of the dream−shrine was smooth as silk, and she found that its texture coaxed her hands to press against the stone that was like none she had encountered in the waking world. A dim light, the source of which she could not ascertain, made it possible for her to see the magnificent artifacts that were all around her, as well as the magnificent carvings on the walls, for she had left her torch lying on the floor at the chamber's entrance. The carvings all depicted squat beasts that crawled on their bellies: turtles, lizards, crocodiles, insects, and such. It felt like a magical place indeed, and Mandy imagined that some of that supernatural essence was seeping from the surface that she touched into the texture of her skin. Could she possess a source of sorcery, she wondered, a power that was in−nate in those of her gender, however much it may be unacknowl−edged and subdued?

She came upon a small and curious mound of dust, in the center of which rested what looked to be the skull of an impossible fiend.

165

Mandy inhaled the fragrance that wafted from the mound and thought of musk incense; and it was when she reached into the mound so as to lift a handful of it to her nostrils that her fingers touched a thing of solid metal, which they clutched and removed from the heap. Even in the chamber's dull light, the golden object shimmered with resplendent hue. Some kind of bracelet, she surmised. Resting it in her palm, Mandy ran her thumb over the curious symbols that had been etched onto the bracelet's surface, sigils that she knew were a kind of language that was unearthly and alien. Outré as the characters seemed, they were superbly formed, and their outline contained an exquisite grace that Mandy found so attractive she wanted to copy it. She patted one edge of the mound so that it became a flat surface, and then she pressed her finger onto that surface and began to copy the characters on the bracelet. From behind her, a faint sound of wind began to bay, and the chamber grew chilly, but the sensation thus created was not unpleasant. Humming a little, Mandy studied the alien letters that she had etched in dust, and the wind behind her seemed to decipher those letters and articulate their language. A whirlwind encased the woman and whirled the small mound, so that its substance rose into the air and formed a semblance. Mandy continued to hum as it formed before her as an antique mummy wrapped in weathered gauze, its bare skull of black bone twitching as the wind's humming filtered through the cavity of the thing's parted jaws.

Stunned by what she had unwittingly called forth merely by inscribing the beautiful characters from the golden bracelet into the dust on the floor, Mandy watched as the mummy's phantom moved its terribly withered limbs, causing the tattered linen wrappings that encased the entity to shred and crumble into particles. The remnant of flesh covering the thing's head was so deteriorated, so dry and cracked and parchment-like, that it could not possibly have any spark of life still in it; but live it did, if only temporarily. The resurrected mummy's blackened skull suddenly swiveled to face her, and its jaws began to work frenetically. A jarring speech issued from that horrible mouth, although no tongue remained behind those broken brown teeth. Mandy quickly realized that she heard its words only in her mind, and not through her ears. The form of language the phantom used was utterly unknown to her, but she somehow understood the essence of its meaning.

"You awaken me from the sleep of centuries. Tell me, what is it you seek in this shrine of the low ones, child?"

Mandy stammered, not having expected she might be questioned by this apparition. "I'm very sorry, sir. I didn't mean to disturb your sleep!"

"That is of no importance. What do you want, child? Tell me without delay, for I do not have long to remain in this form. That which comes from out of dust must return to dust. It is the Law."

"Sorry again, sir! Uh, what I want, what Miss Penelope, the lady I'm here with, wants, is to locate the fortress of the night-gaunts, where we think her brother is being held. Can you tell us where to find it?"

"No. I cannot, for I do not possess that knowledge. But there is an exalted one here who does have that knowledge and will possibly aid you. He awaits, ahead in this shrine. Look for the one who rolls the sun's disk through the sky each day. They call him Khepri."

Mandy was about to ask how she would recognize this Khepri fellow, but she didn't get the chance. The mummy's form began to shimmer—slightly at first and then with great agitation—after which a gust of wind that smelled of spices and incense arose from out of the shadows, swirled around his figure for a few seconds, and blew him away into nothingness, leaving Mandy alone again in the chamber.

Well, perhaps this Khepri would recognize her if she didn't recognize him first, she thought as she crawled along deeper into the chamber. By now, the ceiling was so low that it brushed against the top of her head, scraping her scalp as she made her way down a dimly lit passageway on hands and knees. And then the ceiling became even lower, forcing her to crawl on her stomach like one of the turtles whose images lined the walls in that part of the structure.

Just ahead, some small, humble creature inched across the path.

She stopped to watch it from a safe distance, afraid at first that it might be a spider, but it was not; it was a black beetle that was in the act of laboriously rolling a brownish ball of organic matter that looked like clay laced with straw across the flagstones before her, from right to left.

When the beetle finally had the ball in the very center of the passageway, it turned its whole body toward Mandy, wiggled its an-tennae, then abruptly turned away and began rolling the ball down the path in the same direction that Mandy was headed. Keeping a good space between them, Mandy patiently followed the beetle for what must have been fifteen feet, at which point the low passageway opened up into a much larger space with ceilings so high that Mandy could barely detect them within the deep shadows that accumulated there.

Once they had entered this larger chamber, the mysterious beetle stopped in its tracks and stood motionlessly facing Mandy for several moments, the static ball of what she later learned was dung resting before it. Was this silly bug the great Khepri, of whom the mummy had spoken?

"I am that one," she heard intoned in her mind.

"You're Khepri, who may help us find Jimmy? That's his nick-name. His real name is James."

"I am that one."

She didn't see how a tiny beetle might help solve Penelope's huge problem, but ultimately Mandy had limitless faith, and so she accepted that it could and would help them.

"Okay, Mister Khepri, sir. Where do we find the night-gaunts?"

That was all the deity required: that she show true faith in its potential powers. Given that which it required from any seeker, the beetle stood on its hind legs and wiggled its front legs in the air while its antennae twitched excitedly. As if pulled aside by a powerful magnet, the dung ball rolled away under its own force and came to rest against the chamber wall. While the scarab beetle watched, the dung ball began to tremble and teeter back and forth. A piece of the ball's surface cracked loose and was pushed upward by tiny legs emerging from within the ball. Soon, a newborn infant beetle crawled from out of the dung ball and stumbled a few inches away on fledgling legs. The nascent beetle began to wriggle and writhe as it transformed into a dark, sticky, worm—like figure that swelled and shrank and swelled again until it assumed the shape of a standing man with two arms and two legs; but instead of having a normal human head, this weird being had positioned on its shoulders a shiny black beetle's body where its head should be. Although at first nude, once the ancient deity known as Khepri had fully materialized in his complete human—animal hybrid form, Mandy saw that he was garbed in a long, ornate robe that made him look quite regal.

Finally realizing that she no longer needed to squat down now that they were in a more open chamber, Mandy rose to her feet, not once taking her eyes off the fantastic being before her.

Keeping his hands plunged into the pockets of the robe, the great Khepri swiftly approached Mandy, terrifying her with the suddenness of his movements, until he was only inches away and towering over her. His grotesque beetle—like head completely horrified her. She had never seen such a monstrous thing, and yet, she did not detect any hostility or menace from Khepri, so maybe he was not evil, although he certainly looked it. The shiny black beetle that was his head made high—pitched clicking noises, but she heard no words in her mind in conjunction with this, so she decided that he was not speaking to her at this time but was merely making the typical noises beetles make. And then she did hear his words loudly echoing in her mind.

"The infant I now hand you will lead you and your companion to the night—gaunts," said Khepri.

Pulling his left hand from one of the robe's pockets, she sensed it held some small, precious object which he then gently placed into her open palm. Mandy stared at it in wonder and quickly realized that the gauzy clump of matter was the cocoon of a highly unusual moth. That was, in fact, the chrysalis of her good and noble friend, the magical creature called "The Herald of The Morning."

Chapter XXXV

Clinging tightly to the phosphorescent fur that covered the thorax of the giant moth, Mandy felt completely contented and free, as if she had been born for this alone. The cold wind burned her eyes and made them weep, but hers were tears of joy, not sadness. Her long brown hair whipping wildly behind her while the folds of her flannel nightgown buckled and thrashed in the stiff breeze, Mandy dug her bare heels into the furry sides of the gargantuan creature's abdomen and willed it to fly even faster than it already was. Seated behind her on the moth's broad back, Penelope—terrified by the speed and daring of their flight through this dark, mysterious realm—begged Mandy to slow down, but to no avail.

Neither woman knew how long they had been passing through this vague, nameless domain, racing at feverish speed over its desolate desert floor. Minutes? Hours? There was no way to tell.

"Mandy, for the love of God, will you please take it easy? I can barely hang on!" And barely hanging on Penelope was, her arms wrapped in a crushing bear hug around Mandy's tiny waist and her eyes pressed hard against the girl's back so as to protect herself from wind, and so that she didn't have to watch the ground dizzily rush− ing past them fifty feet below.

"Have you gone completely mad? What in heaven's name is the hurry? It's not as if Jimmy's going anywhere!" But Mandy was a girl possessed, and would not be delayed.

"We'll be there soon!" yelled Mandy over the roar of the wind. "It's just ahead, where that pale amber light glows along the horizon."

"On that big mountain? That's where the night—gaunts have Jimmy?"

"Yes. That's what I have been told by the Herald of the Morning."

"Fantastic. If I'm not present when you arrive, know that I have fallen off somewhere along the way and am lying dead on the desert floor. There's no need to return and bury me. The buzzards will pick my bones clean. Please do inform my coworkers at Miskatonic University Library so they will hire a replacement for me, as I shall not be going back to work, having expired in this infernal place."

"Oh, Penny!" Mandy laughed. "You are such a kidder!"

"I've never been more serious in my life, dear."

As they neared the mountain, it became apparent that the peaks were heavily shrouded in fog. The giant moth rose to a higher elevation and they disappeared into the bank of clouds obscuring the mountaintop. Now they were flying blind, with nothing visible around them but a thick gray mist.

"How do we keep from crashing?" screamed Penelope.

"Don't worry, Penny. The Herald knows the way. He will take us there safely. You must have faith."

"Oh, I have plenty of faith . . . that we'll never get out of this alive!"

Mandy roared with laughter at Penelope's witticisms. "And courage, too," she added. "Courage is essential in this life."

As much as she hated to admit it, Penelope considered that the girl just might be on to something. After all, Mandy had gotten them this far, hadn't she? How far had Penelope's constant cynicism and endless fear ever gotten her? Exactly nowhere. The loss of her little brother so many years ago when she was a young woman at the start of her life had left her a sad, bitter, and timid person who took no risks and expected nothing good from the world. It was a philosophy that hadn't served her well. Maybe she should listen more to Mandy, and do as Mandy suggested once in a while. Maybe she should have faith that this silly giant moth creature would take them to Jimmy as promised. What did she have to lose, really? She decided to quit complaining so much and just wait and see what would happen next.

After a while they slowed down, and it felt as if they were descending. And then the clouds suddenly parted and not far below they saw a hilltop settlement of some kind—an ancient complex built on a flat expanse of mountaintop. A vast network of hundreds of cages with rusted iron bars extended from one edge of the mountaintop to the other, with a grid of walkways separating the cages into rows. Some of the cages were empty, but most held children ranging in age from the littlest of toddlers to big kids who were almost teenagers. Both women knew instantly that this was the night-gaunts' stronghold, the legendary fortress where they held captive the children they had so cruelly abducted.

The Herald of the Morning gracefully touched down atop a wide stone wall on the edge of the complex and came to a rest.

Penelope braced herself, sure that they would be immediately challenged by either night-gaunts or whatever evil beings acted as guards there; but to her tremendous surprise that did not happen. No one rushed forward to question their arrival. No one even came out of the huts that appeared to serve as guard stations. A few nearby children stared at them from behind bars but said nothing, and most of the children didn't even look up to witness their arrival. It was strangely quiet on the hilltop. A few of the children sang nursery rhymes with the softest of voices, but most were silent, and none cried, having depleted their stores of tears long ago.

Mandy slipped off the moth's back, followed by a hesitant Penelope.

"I thought we would be forced to do battle," Mandy said, looking around for someone, anyone that might be in charge of the facility.

"Apparently not," answered Penelope. "Perhaps there are seldom any visitors, and thus no preparations have been made to deal with them."

Mandy shook her head back and forth, negating the suggestion. "I don't think there *are* any guards, not any longer."

She stared at the complex from various perspectives, turning this way and that, reading the historical signs that were hidden in the ancient stones. "I know what's going on here," she finally whispered so as not to arouse notice among the surrounding children. "For countless centuries, the nightgaunts abducted children from all over the waking world and brought them here where, more often than not, they were eventually eaten by the lesser servants of Nodens, Lord of the Great Abyss. They weren't all eaten—it was random, a matter of bad luck. Some children were never touched. Others escaped, and were usually recaptured and returned. And then one day many years ago, the carnage abruptly stopped when the lesser servants of Nodens left this area and relocated to a distant land. The nightgaunts, being mindless creatures of habit, paid no attention to this change and continued to bring their kidnapped victims to the mountaintop and to deposit them in the cages, as they had always done. But the guards stationed here, being much wiser than the nightgaunts, abandoned their posts for good, and thus the children were not watched any more, the cages were no longer locked, and literally nothing kept the children captive here except their own fears. Ever since that day, the children have been free to leave, but few take that opportunity; and when they do, they are almost always caught again by roaming teams of nightgaunts and returned. It's an endless cycle—essentially meaningless, except for the very real tragedy of the children who are lost to their families and almost never seen again by those who love them."

Penelope was stunned. For some moments, she did not know what to say about this bizarre situation. Then the questions began to form in her mind.

"Is Jimmy here?"

"No. he's one of the smarter children, and he always escapes as soon as the nightgaunts leave him here. He wanders the dreamlands, looking for you and your parents, and he gets by okay—he's a clever boy—but they always end up finding him again and bringing him back. He's gotten used to it, actually. It's not a happy existence, but he's not a melancholy child by nature, and so he copes fairly well with his lot in life."

Penelope was keenly disappointed. She had been so excited at the possibility of a reunion with James. Knowing it was hopeless, she nevertheless scanned all the cages, checking each one for his face, but he was not among the captives.

"If we find him again somewhere in dreamland, can I take him back to the waking world?"

"Unfortunately, no. Once children have been taken by the night-gaunts, they cannot return to the waking world of men. It simply is not allowed."

Penelope didn't think to ask who or what forbade these children from going home again.

"So there's nothing for us here, then, nothing we can do to help these children, and no reason to stay any longer—is that correct?"

"Yes," whispered Mandy, sensitive to Penelope's keen disap-pointment. "I'm afraid that's the situation. Let's go now. The waking world awaits us—we who are permitted to return."

And thus they left the dreamland of witchery, riding off on the Herald of the Morning.

Chapter XXXVI

It only took Charles Morelle a few seconds of occupying the body of the aged crone to make the delightful discovery that his psychic perceptions as a witch had been vastly enhanced by exchanging bodies with her. One immediate benefit of his heightened powers was that he intuitively knew what path Rebecca Pascal and her associates had taken when they rode away from the farm on horseback. He also knew that ultimately the party of five would split up, with Poe being the first to separate from the group by flying off on the back of a gargantuan raven, followed by Rebecca and Agnes breaking away from Penelope and Mandy at the threshold of an eldritch city in a desert of white sand. The final thing he foresaw was that the two pairs of women would each enter an ancient temple within the derelict city where they would explore one of three inner temples, with Rebecca and Agnes taking the chamber on the left side while Mandy and Penelope, arriving later, would choose the chamber on the right.

Convinced they were all fools, Charles decided he would explore the middle chamber once he arrived there. The one chamber ignored by the women would surely reward him with unimaginable treasures, for he was obviously far wiser than any of these female dabblers in the black arts. Even the legendary Rebecca Pascal must be an idiot, he reasoned, having gotten her soul eaten by the beast from Outside, Kamog.

Charles wasted no time in leaving the farm to begin retracing their path down the country road on the back of his frustratingly slow pony. By the time he came to the wall of buzzing insects and penetrated it to enter the ancient city, he sensed that the four women had already departed the temple complex. As far as he was concerned, that was a good thing; for he wouldn't need to worry about running into them and having them ask what he—in the semblance of the crone—was doing there.

Keen as it now was, Charles's psychic ability was not all—powerful. There were things about the situation in the temple that he could not detect mentally, one of those being that Agnes had translated the inscription above the middle chamber's entrance as meaning the "Path of Vain Men." Given that he was a very vain man himself, he never once imagined that he might be making a big mistake by entering that particular chamber. And enter it he did, carrying the still smoldering torch that Mandy had earlier tossed aside in his right hand and the crone's cane in his left. The chamber looked inviting enough, although the ceiling was a bit low, which might have been an impediment had he been in his previous male body; but in his present tiny frame, the top of his balding scalp didn't even reach the ceiling tiles above.

Creeping slowly into the dark chamber, shuffling along on gnarled feet while the cane tip scraped dryly at the pavement, Charles saw only a black void ahead, as featureless as dreamless slumber. At fifty feet in, the ceiling gradually began to recede higher and higher until it was no longer visible, and then the stone walls diverged and disappeared into the gloom. He began to get nervous, thinking that by now he ought to have come to something more substantial than this empty, impenetrable darkness—like the door to a treasure vault, or a sarcophagus holding a jewel—laden mummy, or a golden altar bearing a grimoire of forbidden spells. But there was nothing ahead, apparently—just more emptiness. A hint of an odor began to tickle his nostrils: the funky scent of dampness and vegetation. With this dank aroma, the air took on a gray haziness that resolved itself into what he could only call a fog. How could there be fog inside a stone building? Assuming, that is, that he was still inside the temple and hadn't accidentally strayed into a cave system abut—

ting the structure. The fog reflected back the dim ruby glow of his smoldering torch, making it impossible for Charles to see much beyond his extended arm. He noticed that now he was walking on a soft pad of decayed peat, and not a stone floor. Something brushed at his side as he passed it—a thin tree branch.

"Son of a bitch! I'm in the woods," he muttered to no one.

Maybe I should turn back, he thought, but his greed for whatever unknown wonders lay ahead kept him moving forward, the cane sinking into the forest floor as he tapped it rhythmically to steady himself.

And then something emerged from the fog as he approached it: a squarish object, a piece of furniture. It was, he soon saw, an antique vanity table of the kind cluttering bedrooms all over Arkham's older neighborhoods. It had an oval mirror in the center, with a table top below and drawers under that. *What a crazy thing to find in an ancient temple,* he mused. The silvered backing of the mirror was tarnished but not so badly as to deny him a clear view of the bizarre image it reflected. Expecting to see the crone's decrepit form in the glass—shriveled and bent—Charles was stunned by what he viewed instead: the likeness of a beautiful young woman staring back at him. She was the crone, all right, but at twenty years of age and not a century. The woman reflected in the mirror was tall, voluptuous, and sensuous, with an alluring figure and lovely long hair. And—miraculously—she was Charles.

He was delighted with the strangeness of the transformation he had magically undergone and began to imagine all sorts of wild adventures he might have, now that he was possessed of a seductive female body that was brimming with youth and vitality instead of being trapped in the deteriorating flesh of a worn-out hag. This must be the treasure he had sensed awaited him in this middle chamber!

And then Charles noticed lying on the vanity table Rebecca Pascal's scrapbook of clippings and photos from her days as a silent film star. He knew it also held the vintage photographs of those occult creatures, the night-gaunts, that Mandy had brazenly stolen and sold on the black market back in the waking world. Judging it a great prize, he grabbed the scrapbook and pressed it tightly against his bosom.

His joy at these unforeseen gifts did not last long, for as Charles gazed at himself in the mirror, admiring his sexy new figure, imagining to what uses he might put the previously unknown night-gaunt images, a hulking form emerged from out of the fog behind him and fell upon his back with the savage fury of a wild animal. Massive, powerful arms squeezed his rib cage, forcing all the air from his lungs, while something terribly sharp repeatedly slashed at his neck and breasts. The scaly reptilian face he glimpsed in the mirror made no sense to him: half of it was green, the other half purple. The huge hands that tore mercilessly at his flesh had long, razor-sharp claws that penetrated deep and drew blood. The horror of his situation filled his mind; he was being brutally murdered by some monstrous creature of nightmare—his life stolen, his beautiful new body utterly ruined. And there was nothing he could do to stop this outrage.

In a fresh burst of frenzy, the half-human beast struck one last, extremely forceful blow, inflicting a fatal gash across his neck, severing his jugular vein, and then it held him up like a limp rag doll so that he could suffer the indignity of watching himself die in the mirror. Hot scarlet liquid gushed from his neck, streaming in thick rivulets down his breasts and soaking into the pages of Rebecca Pascal's scrapbook. The supreme irony of the situation became his last thought: the hideous scene he was now witnessing in the mirror was exactly the one depicted in the old Mexican movie poster he had wasted so much time examining at the Hobo Bean Coffee Company while lusting after the coeds who ate lunch there. Only this time, the victim of the often-imagined but now genuine violence was not some obscure Latino actress; it was him! Falling forward out of the beast's suddenly relaxed grip, he half dropped, half laid the blood-soaked scrapbook on the vanity table, then collapsed onto the spongy floor of the forest, where he died.

Chapter XXXVII

Sunlight streaming through the windows woke Penelope. She felt dazed and disoriented, as if she had slept for years. She didn't even know what day of the week it was, whether it was a workday or the weekend. The flannel nightgown felt comforting on her warm skin. She closed her eyes and tried to doze a bit longer to savor the luxury of peaceful sleep, but found she couldn't get back to sleep again; for she was sitting slouched down in her grandfather's easy chair, which was comfortable enough for sitting up and reading, but not nearly as cozy for sleeping as being in her own bed, under the covers.

Step into the Moonlight and Other Poems, Rebecca Pascal's slender volume of verse, had fallen from her hands at some time during the night and was now lying ignominiously face down on the floor. She had dreamed about Rebecca last night, and Mandy, and a woman she didn't know named Agnes, along with several other odd people whose names she could not now remember. It had been a long, surreal dream that had made no sense whatsoever, taking place in a bizarre landscape where nothing was as it should be in any well−ordered universe. Mandy had been only a young girl in the dream, but nonetheless had shown an impressive strength of character and an uncommon degree of wisdom as the two of them had struggled mightily to solve some great problem. But what was the problem? She could not recall. It had to do with finding someone or some−thing that was lost. All she knew for certain was that they did not succeed in finding that which they had sought; and yet, it still felt like a good dream, almost a happy dream.

She had not realized what a fine person Mandy truly was: a kind, decent, honest woman, uncommonly unselfish, and smart, too. She had always known where to go, who to talk to, and what to do in every situation, while Penelope had invariably felt hopelessly lost. Something about Mandy's unassuming innocence and openness in the dream made Penelope want to dig out the notebooks she had kept when she was a precocious young girl. In them Penelope had written down everything she had learned about the world's myster-ies, recording every fascinating scrap of hidden history she had gleaned from her voluminous reading. She, too, had once been a bright, positive young girl, just as Mandy was in the dream. She longed to see those notebooks again, and to remember what she once had been, and perhaps might be once more, if she made the effort. She would look for them later in the day—after work, if it was a workday, or after breakfast, if it was Saturday or Sunday.

The warm morning sun felt good on her face. With her eyes shut, still trying without success to doze off, the bright light of the sun made the translucent flesh of her eyelids glow a brilliant red hue. It was going to be a lovely day, she decided, and Penelope looked forward to it with an enthusiasm for life she had not felt for a long, long time. Maybe she would invite Mandy out to lunch and tell her all about her wild dream last night. Mandy might get a kick out of hearing how the two of them had ridden through fantastic, alien skies on the back of a giant phosphorescently glowing moth named . . . what was its name? She could not exactly remember, but it was a strange, beautiful name that had something to do with the morning. Penelope opened her eyes, smiled, and bravely faced the day.

★

Mandy awoke face down in bed, spread out on top of the blan-kets, with some hard object pressing uncomfortably into her stomach muscles. She pulled it out from underneath her and stared at it in numb confusion until she realized it was the book of poems by Edith Gnome. She had fallen asleep reading the antique volume, and slept all night with it knocking around on the bed. Now the binding was bent and the pages crumpled as a result of the mistreatment to which she had subjected it. Oh well, it was the library's book, so what did she care if it was damaged? But then again, maybe she would do something that, for her, would be very uncharacteristic; report the damage and pay the fine. Something about last night's long, weird dream made her feel as if she ought at least to try to be a more honest person than she had been so far in life.

That nice older lady, Penelope, had been in the dream, and Mandy had been doing her utmost to help Penny accomplish some difficult task in what was a very difficult and confusing environment. She didn't remember very much about the dream, but she had come away from it with the feeling that they had not been successful in achieving their goal; but in the end it hadn't really mattered much, because at least they had sincerely tried to do the right thing, and in the dream Mandy had felt quite proud of herself for having made a concerted effort to help Penelope do the difficult thing, whatever it was.

She realized there were a lot of things she could change to make her life better, to be a better person. Like stop stealing from Miskatonic's library. She was all done with that craziness. She resolved that from now on she would simply do her job as a book conservator, be honest, obey the rules, and focus on being the best person she could be. A life of petty crime had not made her happy. Perhaps a life of service to others would. There was no harm in trying, was there? She still had time to change her ways. No one except that evil Doctor Lang knew about the photos she'd stolen, and he wouldn't dare tell anyone about them if he wanted to keep out of trouble himself. That annoying graduate student, Charles Morelle, was vaguely aware that Mandy had taken the photos and sold them to Lang, but that was all hearsay on his end—he had no real proof. Yes, she would turn over a new leaf, as they say. She would be a good person from now on. That was a very appealing idea.

Rising from the bed, she went to the window, threw open the curtains, and looked out at the glowing sunrise, the light of which shimmered in her enchanted eyes. Arkham was beautiful when the golden light of morning washed away the sinister gloom of night; and yet that daylight contained a rare quality, and to feel it wash over one was to feel that it was the magical light of Arkham that made the town's ominous shadows possible—and all the fantastic things that may dwell within those shadows. For this was a witch-town, and Mandy was anxious to return to work on restoring the scrapbook of Arkham's most amazing enchantress, Rebecca Pascal. Was today a workday? Mandy hoped that it was, for there was much work to be done, and she was the one to do it. And after that work was accomplished, she could sink again into the realm of dream, and thus continue her miraculous adventures with Arkham's remarkable sorceress.

Chapter XXXVIII

Agnes stopped to look at the moon as she and Rebecca neared the black mountain; and she marveled that the sphere was more magical than she had ever seen it, that its shadows seemed to darken and engulf the sphere as she watched. Rebecca, seeming to have read the other woman's mind, spoke.

"You know, of course, that there are three distinct aspects of what we call 'shadow.' There is umbra, penumbra, and antumbra. The ironic thing about shadow is that it requires light in order to exist. Well, at least in the waking world. The shadows in this dreamland of witchery are subject to other laws, and they are manifestations of their own kind. Look at how that moon shifts in tone and is now a sphere between the shades of cobalt and magenta. This is how the moon appears when one nears Mount K'Nath. Can you sense how the ground trembles slightly underfoot? The mountain is restless, sensing our presence. Ah, let's rest beside this pool."

Rebecca's words were weighty with a kind of alchemy, and Agnes found that she could not resist the spell they wove inside her mind. She sank onto one of the large stones that bordered the pool, and then she leaned forward a little to gaze into the obscurity within the dark water, where liquid shadows coiled.

"I'm so tired," Agnes moaned. "It's like I'm oppressed with an enormous weight—as if that mountain had been fastened to my back. God, it has just as much presence as Mount Selta in Sesqua Valley—but of a more somber kind." Her eyes grew a little brighter, and she straightened up. "What is it about this dreamland? I've been

185

trying to figure it out. It has a bleak and morbid tone, an aura of pitch. Any kind of light that exists here seems warped and slightly thwarted. Unlike the light in Sesqua, which is majestic and sublime! I don't belong here. This place makes me so dizzy."

As if the word proved too suggestive, Agnes began to tilt toward the pool as her eyes grew heavy. Rebecca's hands shot forward and caught those of the younger woman, and Agnes was pulled away from the pool, to a spot of cool earth. She lifted her hands to her face and began to rub it, and then she gasped a little and began to run her hands over the ground.

"What on earth is the matter, dear?" spoke Rebecca's sly voice.

"I had the Key of Shadow in this hand. I must have dropped it!" She began to push herself up on her knees, but stopped at the sound of Rebecca's playful laughter.

"You haven't lost it, my dear. It's right here."

"Oh, please give it back. I promised Edith that I'd bring it to her. That's why she sent me here."

The elder woman chortled. "That paltry trickster who dares to think herself a witch? Pah! She was too spineless to enter this dreamland herself, because she knew she would have to contend with me. So she sent her little shadow—girl, and you have stumbled from folly to folly. Neither of you deserve the power of this key. Neither of you realize its uses. With it I can unlock a multitude of doorways—perhaps even to the waking world itself."

"You don't *exist* in the waking world. You have no body to re—turn to. If anyone is a shadow—girl, it's you!"

The hand was swift that slapped Agnes, and she held up her arms to guard her head should a second blow come forth. Instead, Rebecca stood before her, a creature of lunatic determination.

"It's true that I have squandered my mortal soul and my magnificent body to that foul fiend, Kamog. Yet if mortal flesh has a way to cross the border into dreamland, as has been done before, then it may be possible for a denizen of dreamland to find a pathway into the waking world. The night—gaunts have learned the trick; and there are two points in dreamland that cross into the realm of reality, as it is foolishly called by some. Perhaps I can exist in the waking world as a thing of shadow only, but I am determined to find a way back—in any guise. Now that I possess this key, there may be no limit to what I can accomplish. I leave you to the shadows that crowd around you. Try not to be afraid."

Turning from her, Rebecca sauntered to the mountain wall, to which she touched one end of the Key of Shadow. A portion of the rock before her grew denser with darkness, and without turning to taunt Agnes further, the actress stepped into the void and passed its threshold.

Agnes expected to feel fear, and was surprised to find that she felt dull anger instead. "I won't be afraid, bitch," she spat toward the place where Rebecca had vanished. "I'm an enchantress from Sesqua Valley, and I carry the valley's alchemy with me wherever I may be hurled."

Agnes began to realize, more and more, the reason that Edith sent her to this awful place: so as to find her true power, her authentic self. She rose unsteadily to her feet. Shutting her eyes, she called with every fiber of her being to Sesqua Valley. A glow began to taint the surface of her eyelids. Opening her eyes, Agnes saw that rays of shimmering radiance were rising from the water in the pool. Stumbling to the pool, she looked on its surface and saw the source of light—a bright sphere that she recognized as the sun over Sesqua Valley. She became aware of the fragrance in the fumes that floated upward from the water, and knew that it was the pungent sweetness that existed in the valley's aether. Intoxicated, she stood atop one of the huge rocks that formed the pool's border, and then she stepped from that rock, into liquid depths.

Her eyes had closed again, and the surface of her eyelids still held the light and warmth of valley sunlight. A small dry hand smoothed her hair, and an ancient voice called her name.

"Stir yourself, Agnes Aspinwall. Return to the waking world." Edith Gnome's frail arms wrapped around her, and with their aid Agnes was able to get on her knees in the meadow of soft grass. The sight of the elderly woman so affected her that Agnes broke into a fit of sobbing. "There, there, sweetheart. You're safe with friends."

"Edith, Edith! I had the key, that awful emblem. But I lost it to Rebecca, and heaven knows what use she'll make of it!"

A trace of sadness clouded the old woman's eyes; but then she smiled and, holding the younger woman's hand, helped them both to their feet. "Not to worry, Agnes. Perhaps it is all for the best. It may be that Sesqua Valley is all the dreamland that I need."

A strange bestial cry came from somewhere among the peaks of Mount Selta, causing Agnes to gaze toward that majestic white titan. Her attention was caught by a figure that leaned against a tree at the distant place where the woodland of the valley began, and her heart began to beat a faster pace. Although the person was hid in shadow, his persona was inescapable. Simon Gregory Williams returned her gaze; and then he raised a sleek flute to his mouth and filled the valley with eerie song.

— FINIS —